"Anybody ever tell you you got tough-looking legs?"

I waited until he was gone and then bent to take a quick objective look at my legs. People were always talking about my keen mind and contagious smile and dedicated social conscience, but nobody had in fact ever come right out and told me I had tough-looking legs. I'd have to remember to tell Earl that one. He would get a huge kick, I figured, out of Truck Hardy telling me I had tough-looking legs . . .

A LONG WAY HOME FROM TROY

BANTAM PATHFINDER EDITIONS

A comprehensive and fully integrated series designed to meet the expanding needs of the young adult reading audience and the growing demand among readers of all ages for paperback books of high quality.

Bantam Pathfinder Editions provide the best in fiction and nonfiction in a wide variety of subject areas. They include novels by classic and contemporary writers; vivid, accurate histories and biographies; authoritative works in the sciences; collections of short stories, plays and poetry.

Bantam Pathfinder Editions are carefully selected and approved. They are presented in a new and handsome format, durably bound and printed on specially selected high-quality paper.

A LONG WAY
HOME FROM TROY
Donia Whiteley Mills

BANTAM PATHFINDER EDITIONS
TORONTO / NEW YORK / LONDON

A NATIONAL GENERAL COMPANY

*This low-priced Bantam Book
has been completely reset in a type face
designed for easy reading, and was printed
from new plates. It contains the complete
text of the original hard-cover edition.*
NOT ONE WORD HAS BEEN OMITTED.

RLI: VLM 6 (VLR 4–6) / IL 8–adult

A LONG WAY HOME FROM TROY
*A Bantam Book / published by arrangement with
The Viking Press, Inc.*

*PRINTING HISTORY
Viking edition published November 1971
Bantam Pathfinder edition published November 1972
2nd printing*

Let It Be Me ("*Je T'Appartiens*"). English lyric by Mann Curtis, French lyric by Pierre Delanoe, music by Gilbert Becaud. © Copyright 1955, 1957, 1960 by France Music Co., New York Sole Selling Agent MCA Music, a division of MCA, INC., 445 Park Avenue, New York, N.Y. 10022. International Copyright Secured. Used by Permission. All Rights Reserved.

If I Were a Carpenter by Tim Hardin. © Copyright 1966 by Koppelman-Rubin Enterprises, Inc., New York, N.Y. Permission granted by Publisher.

*All rights reserved.
Copyright © 1971 by Donia Whiteley Mills.
This book may not be reproduced in whole or in part, by
mimeograph or any other means, without permission.
For information address: The Viking Press, Inc.,
625 Madison Avenue, New York, N.Y. 10022.*

Published simultaneously in the United States and Canada

Bantam Books are published by Bantam Books, Inc., a National General company. Its trade-mark, consisting of the words "Bantam Books" and the portrayal of a bantam, is registered in the United States Patent Office and in other countries. Marca Registrada. Bantam Books, Inc., 666 Fifth Avenue, New York, N.Y. 10019.

PRINTED IN THE UNITED STATES OF AMERICA

For JVG

Chapter 1

To this day I don't know why he picked *me* to swoop down on that April afternoon. Roaring up in his incredible tank of a car that would have given me the creeps sitting in a church parking lot, not to mention on a deserted stretch of Bentley Road.

Too classy for sidewalks, Bentley Road was. If you were walking you had a choice between the road itself or the spongy sod of well-kept lawns, with the houses all sitting remotely back behind the trees. I had chosen the road that day, walking home from school minding my own business, when suddenly this shiny black-and-white car with fat rear tires roars up out of nowhere and skids to a sensational halt beside me.

"No, thanks anyway!" I called out to the guy, who couldn't possibly have heard me above the radio wailing, "Mayeek thuh wurrrrrrrrld go away, and git it awfuh mah shoulderzzzzzz!" He reached over and turned it down maybe a fraction of a decibel.

"What's that?"

"I say, I'm almost home, thanks anyway," I shouted, resisting the urge to break into a dead run. I wasn't normally the chicken type, but there wasn't another soul in sight and it was getting on toward the dinner hour and this guy happened to be the biggest hood in the whole school. I wasn't normally walking home alone so late either, except that particular day I had to stay after for a last-minute meeting of the Slave Auction Committee. That was our big charity event of the year, to raise money for sending underprivileged kids to Camp Manahocket. They auctioned off the cheerleaders and a bunch of other student leaders and then on Slave Day whoever bought them made them dress up in funny clothes and do crazy stuff around the school. Typical sort of thing I was always getting roped into.

"What's the matter, you think I bite or something?"

Despite Albemarle's Ivy League image we did have a small black-leather-jacket colony, known not too affectionately as the "greasers." Except this one's leather jacket was brown. His name was Truck Hardy, and he had a pack of Lucky Strikes on the dashboard and an angel dangling from his rearview mirror. A white plastic angel, of all things, with stiff feathered wings spread out as if in perpetual blessing. *Bless you, my son, bless you, bless you. Now why don't you just go away?*

"Or maybe you're just one of those fresh-air freaks, that it? Tell you what, I'll roll down all the windows and you can pedal."

I assured him that my home was close by, whereupon he offered to drive along beside me to make sure I got there safely. Really noble, like the wolf volunteering to be Red Riding Hood's bodyguard.

I also had on a very short skirt, a detail he had not failed to notice.

"Just hate to see that tough-looking pair of legs get tuckered out, that's all. Anybody ever tell you you got tough-looking legs?"

I thought perhaps if I walked a little faster.

"How come you're so stuck on yourself, huh? Cause you're going steady with that Corbett jock?"

I flashed him a desperate, *oh-come-now* smile, at which point the load of books I was carrying began to jog loose.

"If I was a big jock, would you go steady with me?"

First the trig book, flipping onto the pavement with a noisy *splat*. Then when I bent to pick that up, a sheaf of Student Council announcements slipped out the bottom of my notebook, followed by a yellow Magic Marker and my beloved dog-eared copy of the latest Mount Holyoke College catalogue.

"I mean, Honor Society and this club and that club and a cheerleader besides and wooooo-EEEE! Wish I had me a big old wheel like that in *my* garage."

By some miracle I finally made it home. To be decent about it, I did step over to the car to bid him farewell. Up close he didn't look quite as raunchy as he sounded —if a cross between Johnny Cash and Tarzan appeals to you, with a little Warren Beatty thrown in around the eyes.

"Change your mind?"

"No, this is where I live. Thanks anyway."

"Tough life." He leaned across the seat and looked our spread over like a prospective buyer. White frame and gray stone, twin willows flanking the driveway. "You sure got it made, don't you, sugar?"

I didn't take this question too seriously, which worked out pretty well since he didn't hang around for an answer. He just told me to "Be good, now," gave me a cozy wink, put his machine in gear, and screeched off, laying a generous patch of rubber.

I waited until he was gone and then bent to take a quick objective look at my legs. People were always talking about my keen mind and contagious smile and dedicated social conscience, but nobody had in fact ever come right out and told me I had tough-looking legs. I'd have to remember to tell Earl that one. He would get a huge kick, I figured, out of Truck Hardy telling me I had tough-looking legs. With this thought in mind, I bounced into the house and back to the kitchen to discover, contrary to the opinion of Truck Hardy and the rest of the world, that I did not quite have it made after all.

The refrigerator door, for obvious reasons, was where my mother always left my mail. She secured the envelopes with little magnets shaped like pieces of fruit. As long as I live I shall recall the vision of that letter from Mount Holyoke riveted there that afternoon with a tiny pineapple. Without even opening it she had steaks marinating and wine chilling, a good example of my mother's blind faith in Alumnae Power.

She had gone to Mount Holyoke herself (cum laude, '45) and certainly must have been one of their most loyal graduates of all time. I guess it was inevitable that I would fall under the Holyoke spell the way I did. Ever since I was six years old I'd been dressed in Holyoke sweat shirts, entertained with Holyoke yearbooks and alumnae brochures, and otherwise steered enthusiastically in the direction of South Hadley, Massachusetts. And of course there was the indisputable fact, nestling somewhere in the middle of all this, that Mount Holyoke was an outstanding college in every way. By the time I had reached my senior year the brainwashing was complete: I didn't even have any second choice, only a couple of "just in case" schools where I finally applied halfheartedly at my father's insistence.

From the beginning, Albemarle's college counselor had assured me that I should have no problem getting into Holyoke, with my good grades and lengthy record of school activities. There was the small matter of my board scores, which were not exactly crowding eight hundred—but after all, insisted my parents and teachers and friends, shouldn't a well-rounded personality and diligent study habits more than make up for a sub-genius IQ?

I'm not going to go into the morbid details of how I opened the letter and unfolded it and read it and stared out the window in utter dismay and then read it again and finally held it out numbly to my mother standing there waiting with a sack of charcoal and a look of eager anticipation. All I'm going to say is, there must be a more humane way of putting it than "waiting list." If they tell you "yes," you can rejoice, and if they tell you "no," at least you can throw yourself across your bed and have a good cry. But when they assure you that your qualifications are excellent and they would like very much to make you a part of their freshman class, however they regret that there are at present no openings due to lack of space so they are placing your name on a waiting list and you will be notified immediately in turn should sufficient openings occur, what can you say?

"Now, if that isn't the strangest thing," were my mother's first words, delivered with a faint, disbelieving smile. "Somebody must have made a mistake somewhere along the line."

"I don't think so," I said slowly. "I don't think Holyoke makes mistakes. Holyoke just has about five hundred fantastically qualified applicants for every opening, is what I think. With all their board scores in the high seven hundreds. Verbal *and* math."

"Well, in any case, you're probably right at the top of this waiting list," she said. "All you have to do is wait until a few of their acceptances decide to go somewhere else."

"Somewhere *else!* Nobody accepted there wants to go anywhere else, Mother! Holyoke is not exactly a second-choice school."

"Oh, you never know, Jeannette. Things happen sometimes. Maybe somebody will run away to Cuba or get pregnant or something." She straightened my collar and gave me a consoling little squeeze before stepping outside to brush the grill and start the fire. "It could be worse."

I didn't think so. I didn't think there could be anything worse than running second-string with a good possibility of being cut altogether. I sat down at the kitchen table and read those two scant paragraphs over and over to see if there wasn't some subtle nuance I hadn't seen before, some faint note of hope or encouragement, anything but the prospect of renewed anxiety with no end in sight.

I was still sitting there staring at the crisp typewritten words when Earl arrived, fresh from track practice and a hot shower, for traditional Friday night dinner with the Travises.

"Boo," he said, appearing suddenly in the kitchen doorway. "Hey." He came over and gave me a weak punch on the arm. "I saw your mom out on the patio, she told me the news. I know how you feel, but don't panic yet. I'm sure everything will work out eventually. You'll just have to take it in stride."

Typical Earl Corbett advice: don't panic, take it in stride. And how did he know how I felt, anyway? *I* wasn't even sure how I felt. It was just so beautifully ironic, was the thing. *Waiting list.* After all those grades sweated, books read, facts memorized, cheers led, campaigns battled, all that toeing the line.

I watched him as he sank into the chair beside me, stretched out his long legs, and picked up my trig book from the table.

"You do number six on this page yet? It's a real stinker."

"I haven't even made it to number one."

"Wait'll you get to six."

About this time my father came bustling in the back door—loosening his tie, slapping his *Wall Street Journal* down on the counter—to mix himself a martini before dinner. The fire was white-hot and ready, he informed us with a glance at his watch. The steaks should be done in about twelve and a half minutes.

"How about those Senators, huh?" he said to Earl. "Getting Marsh *and* that rookie Benzell from St. Louis, for Hallister."

"Fantastic," Earl agreed. "Hallister can't hit his way out of a paper bag any more."

"Earl," I said, "you want to go in the den and work on these trig problems for twelve and a half minutes?"

"Sure thing, Jeannie. I'll be in there in just a sec."

My father was looking in the refrigerator for olives. "Now all we have to worry about is a shortstop."

"Boy, you said it there. You think anything'll ever come of this Altizer deal?"

Bleakly, I excused myself and went in to set the table.

My father was a jolly man, pudgy and balding and doing extremely well in something called Management Consultation. Which meant, roughly speaking, that it was his daily business to ferret out and solve the huge weighty problems of multimillion-dollar corporations. It is easy to see how it might strike him as no big deal that I had been placed on the waiting list of the college of my choice.

"I know a couple of people up there," he said at dinner, carving medium-rare sirloin into hefty portions. "If you'd like, I'll check around a little and see what I can find out."

"Thank you, Daddy, that would be very nice, but I don't think pulling strings is any way to get into a place like Mount Holyoke."

"Who said anything about pulling strings?" my mother asked soothingly, pouring us all another round of sparkling burgundy.

Earl, munching salad, ventured the opinion that it wasn't safe to bank on any one school as a sure thing these days, considering such factors as open admissions, geographical distribution, et cetera, over which one had no control. "I mean, do you have any idea how many kids from the D.C. area are applying to the Ivy League schools? You shouldn't feel bad, Jeannie—it's just all this local competition. If you were from Kansas or somewhere, with your record, Holyoke would snap you up just like that."

My parents agreed.

"So what am I supposed to do, move to Kansas?"

"Honestly," my mother said. "I'm sure she's right at the top of this waiting list. All she has to do is be patient a little while longer."

"Pass the salt, please?" my father said.

I don't mean to give the impression that my parents were piggish or insensitive; they just tended to look on the positive side of things endlessly, which can sometimes become a strain. To be honest about it, if you made a survey of all the parents in our group, mine probably would have won the prize for fair and liberal treatment of offspring. The latter was mostly my dad's influence—like allowing beer at parties ("Better to let them drink it here than out parked in some car, Edith") and letting me set my own curfews ("She'll find out for herself the value of a good night's sleep, Edith").

It wasn't until I started dating Earl, back around Thanksgiving, that my mother was finally satisfied with the maturity of my judgment. She was crazy about Earl Corbett. She seemed to sense, with hawklike motherly intuition, that her daughter was in good hands with this young man. The biggest problem with Earl, as she often remarked, was not getting to see nearly enough of him. He was always "in training." He played right end during football season, forward on the basketball team, and specialized in hurdles and the 440-yard dash all spring long. In his bedroom he had clippings from the school and county newspapers all over his walls.

That's the kind of thing Earl Corbett lured a girl up to his bedroom for, to look at his sports clippings.

Also there was the Yale thing. Yale was the masculine equivalent of Mount Holyoke in our family history. My father had gone there and my brother Ben was currently a sophomore there. When Earl was accepted at both Princeton and Yale and chose Yale, this immediately skyrocketed him to the status of permanent family member.

"Won't it be cozy next year?" my mother said once. "With Ben and Earl at Yale and you at Holyoke?"

Which brings me back to the thorny subject at hand.

"Of course it wouldn't hurt to think about other schools. For instance, the ones that accepted you," my father said. "I could give Tom Bradley a call first thing in the morning."

I'd been waiting for that one. He was referring to Darcey College, a small and new and rather experimental school in some dinky town down in Virginia where his old Yale buddy Tom Bradley was Dean of Students. At least they had a coed dorm, he reminded me by way of consolation, and a winter work-study term. They had also accepted me sight unseen, which convinced me it couldn't be much of a place.

"I've been thinking, maybe I won't go to college at all next year," I said. It was the first time the possibility had ever entered my head, but it did sound dramatic enough to stop conversation for a few seconds. "I could go out West, work on a ranch or something." I had never even been on a horse except those Shetlands at carnivals, and mine usually went backward or tried to sit down, but nevertheless I had this stubborn vision of myself as a cowgirl which always cropped up in moments of stress—*Jeannie Travis riding the range, rugged and enduring as the tumbleweed.* You might say I had an overly active romantic imagination, too. Along with the tough-looking legs and the contagious smile and the not-quite-keen-enough mind.

"We'll see," my mother said. Adding that if I didn't want the rest of my steak, perhaps Earl would like to have it. With beef prices the way they were, it was a crime to waste a good steak. Not that the money mattered, she said quickly, it was just the idea of it.

Earl, accepting the offer only after making sure nobody else wanted it, suggested that I ought to at least go down on the bus and visit Darcey one of these weekends, since I had never even seen the place. "How do you know you won't end up loving it?"

My father agreed.

Having solved my problem to everyone's satisfaction, we then had dessert.

After this harrowing day the last thing I felt like doing was triple-dating in Earl's VW bug to a foreign film, but Earl pointed out that there was no sense sitting around moping, right? So we went to the foreign film.

"Hey, in all the excitement I forgot to tell you how it went at practice today," he said as we headed over to Walnut Woods to pick up his best buddy Mick Morton, who happened to have a date that night with my best buddy Trisha Sewall.

"How did it go at practice today?"

"Fifty-two three."

"What's that?"

"The 440. I did the 440 in fifty-two three."

"Wow. You certainly are getting there."

"Coach says if I really work at it there's no doubt I'll be able to hit the fifty-second mark before the season's over. Oh yeah, and he's making me anchor man in the mile relay tomorrow, moving Brunhalter to third."

"Great," I said, smiling blankly at his strong-jawed profile.

After we picked up Mick and Trisha we whipped across the parkway to get Eric Freeman, who was waiting for us out front on the curb, smoking something that looked pretty suspicious. His old man had confiscated his car keys again, he explained in rather colorful language on the way down to pick up Susan Weintraub in Fox Meadow Acres. No foxes, no meadows, just lots of fifty-thousand-dollar houses built four to the acre.

About this time of the year most everyone was in advanced stages of Senior Slump, that lame-duck ailment peculiar to second-semester seniors. Especially at a place like Albemarle, one of those suburban pressure cookers that aren't so much high schools as racetracks for getting into college. They practically put it on the school crest that *89% of our graduates continue on to higher education!*

This was not exactly an accident. As far back as the ninth grade they had begun bombarding everybody with catalogues and pep talks and dire threats about "buckling down." Around Albemarle you were considered disadvantaged if you hadn't taken PSAT, SAT, and achievement tests half a dozen times. Not to mention Kuder Preference Tests, in case it might be the awful truth that you would feel more comfortable (1) building a wooden footstool with your hands than (2) solving calculus problems or (3) reading a volume of Browning's poetry.

Naturally, after a solid year of this madness—college boards, campus visits, essays of approximately 250 words on "What I hope to gain from a college education"—there just isn't much to keep the weary senior plugging once the goal line is crossed. No longer can anyone cow him with threats like, "If you don't get an A in history you probably won't get into Duke." Simultaneously, spring stretches out before him in lazy splendor. School becomes merely a place to go and meet friends five days a week, filled with minor annoyances like teachers who pretend that grades still matter. He develops sudden weaknesses for things like clouds and flowers, deafening volumes of electric guitars, irrational romance.

Except for Earl, of course, who was immune to any kind of slump. And then there was me, with my own unique complication.

When I finally managed to mumble the news to Trisha, bouncing stoically along city streets wedged between her knees and the gearshift, she was genuinely sympathetic. No helpful logic, but lots of loyalty.

"Aw, Jeannie," she said. "I really can't believe that. Some computer up there must have goofed, don't you think? Blown a fuse or something."

Good old Trisha. You couldn't help liking her, she was so simple and honest and uncomplicated. Her idea of a good school was one with a high ratio of boys to girls. For the first time ever, I kind of envied her. Since she also happened to be fairly bright when she wanted to be, she had been accepted at Penn, which had an impressive total of three thousand male undergraduates. Knowing Trisha, you had to figure it would take that many for her to find one who suited her. With Mick Morton, for instance—she'd been chasing him for two months, then as soon as he gave up and started asking her out, she decided she wasn't really that wild about Mick Morton. Who she was *really* wild about was Peter Hoffman. As if that hadn't happened thirty-five times already since the seventh grade.

Eric and Susan, on the other hand, were madly in love and totally wrapped up in each other. I kind of envied them, too. That night they were beset by a couple of minor crises, such as, Eric's old man was not going to give him back his car keys until he got his hair cut, and Susan's parents were going to kick her out of the house if she didn't stop dating Eric. I noticed they weren't letting this adversity spoil their evening, however, since they curled up in a corner of the back seat and made out all the way downtown, disentangling only when we hit the streets of Georgetown.

We had almost half an hour before the show to spend wandering up and down the main strip, looking at weird things in shop windows and checking out various little clusters of activity. Eric and Susan immediately took off down a side street and caught up with us a few minutes later waving a Baggie full of grass.

"Hey, keep it out of sight, will you?" Earl said. "I got a track meet tomorrow. I don't want to spend all night bailing you out of jail."

Although nobody worried too much about keeping anything out of sight in Georgetown. There were literally hundreds of kids milling around the sidewalks—real freaks and pseudo-freaks and suburban runaways and straight types of every description—smoking, tripping, panhandling, loving their neighbors, and just generally being on hand in case something entertaining should happen.

The whole scene had always intrigued me—the unsettling reality of all these people my age living such carefree, day-to-day lives, totally uninterested in traditional education or careers or goals. I looked at the faces flowing by and tried to imagine how they felt, tried to picture myself among them. Saying to hell with the college hassle once and for all, coming down to join the liberated throng—*Jeannie Travis cruising the streets in frayed jeans and Navy pea jacket, long hair swinging, following every impulse that comes along!*

But the simple fact was that the old Protestant ethic clung to me like flypaper: I was a creature of order and direction. And besides, I really wanted to be a teacher. It wasn't any whim of the moment, either. As far back as the sixth grade, when my friends wanted to be actresses and fashion models and newspaper reporters, I wanted to be a schoolteacher. There was something about kids that really knocked me out. And in all the times I'd worked with them, from Trojanette tutoring projects to summer camping jobs, I'd never found myself bored. Harried, unsure of the answers to all their questions—but never bored. I figured there weren't a whole lot of professions around that offered that kind of guarantee—duties varied and materials forever changing and the product renewing itself every day.

"Got any spare change?" a voice said suddenly, bringing me back to the not-so-golden present. A pale, frizzy-haired girl was standing in front of us on the sidewalk, scanning us with quick, determined eyes. When nobody said anything right away she moved on down the theater line, her limp peasant skirt flopping around her legs. "Got any spare change?"

You had to admire their nerve if nothing else, I thought, watching her cross the street and join a group of bearded, barefooted guys on the other side. I wondered if I would ever muster up that kind of nerve in my whole life, the courage to cut loose from an old groove without any real assurance that the new one was going to turn out any better.

"Two, please," Earl said at the ticket window, beaming down at me with a big all-purpose smile.

He was so good-looking.

As for the film, it was in Polish with English subtitles, some sort of political allegory with religious overtones. Not exactly the kind of thing I could get emotionally involved in at the moment. Furthermore, I was the one who got stuck sitting next to Eric and Susan, who continued to make out all during the movie. That really killed me, since it was Eric's idea to go to this foreign flick in the first place.

For comfort or security or something I leaned over in Earl's direction, a move which he misinterpreted as a desire for popcorn. Generously, he offered me his box.

Oh, *Earl,* I lamented—sitting there so serenely absorbed in this Polish saga—Earl Earl Earl Earl. I wished he could just be absorbed in *me* for a change, without parents, without a dozen other people, without administration-approved school functions and stands full of cheering fans. After he had finished the popcorn I edged over in his direction again, and this time he got the message. He put his arm around me warmly, which was the most encouraging thing that had happened all day.

Maybe we could go straight home after the movie, I thought. Just Earl and me. Make something hot to drink, take it down to the rec room. We could put the new José Feliciano album on the stereo, build a little fire in the fireplace. It was April, but maybe we could build a little fire anyway. And just talk it all out, for as long as it took, until I could make some sense out of the whole crazy day.

Unfortunately, things didn't quite work that way. After the movie Trisha insisted on the six of us going to Bernelli's to get a "Mississippi Steamboat," one of their gigantic group-sized ice cream and whipped cream creations. And by the time we had made the return rounds dropping everybody off, it was much too late for him to stay even a minute, Earl said, giving me a few brisk kisses in the foyer.

"I've got a track meet tomorrow, remember? I should've been in bed two hours ago as it is!"

So I ended up communing with faithful old Stanley, whose sagging jowls and sad basset-hound eyes almost made me feel better. He was curled up on the foot of my bed as always, just at the right spot to make a warm place for my feet.

"Poetic justice," I said. Stanley agreed. It must be somebody's idea of poetic justice, my turn coming round at last. My own private taxation for having gotten every single thing in life I'd ever wanted, Peter Max bedspread and my own Princess phone, this club and that club and a cheerleader besides. I didn't really want all that stuff, I just got it. What I really wanted, I didn't even know.

When I have crazy dreams I usually don't remember them very well, but that night was a curious exception. I dreamed I was out West somewhere, working on a ranch. My job was to ride around on a horse and mend the fences. At one place there was a small break in the fence where one cow had managed to squeeze through, then another cow, which made the break even bigger, so that a whole lot of other cows could then go through, and I rode up just in time to see all the cows escaping, stampeding through the fence in a great flying wedge, and I was riding around on that horse bawling my eyes out because all the cows were gone and I didn't know what to do.

Chapter 2

"Now here is a prize fit for a king," breathed auctioneer Ozzie Rosen into the mike as he drew me forward. I climbed up obediently onto the cafeteria-table auction block draped with the exhortation: "Let's All Sock It to Manahocket." "Or maybe a duke or an earl." They all loved that, naturally. Especially Earl, standing in the front row, smiling proudly with Trisha beside him.

I guess I was smiling too, since half the student body was there and I have always made it a point to look cheerful when appearing before large crowds. Actually I was suffering from a slight inferiority complex about having to follow big handsome Dale Hutchins, who had just been sold to a bunch of giggly freshman girls for twenty-nine dollars, the biggest take of the afternoon.

"Five dollars," Earl called out, and Oz pretended anguish.

"Five dollars, the man said. Five measly green ones. Ladies and gents, I say that is an insult to this fair creature. What do you say?"

Somebody upped it to five-fifty, and Earl bid six. Oz rambled on in true auctioneer style, cataloguing all my talents and virtues as a potential slave. Overdoing it a little, I thought. Probably to compensate for my recent ill fortune. Getting wait-listed by the college of one's choice was nothing to sneeze at, after all.

Everyone was being most kind to me—even Earl. He had already outlined his plans for me on Slave Day. First I would cook him and his friends a light breakfast, then drive them to school a little early, so I would have time before class to go around picking up trash off the football field with a poke-stick. Then, at lunch, I was to wander around the cafeteria with a petition calling for more humane treatment of us poor, downtrodden slaves. All in all, not a terribly strenuous schedule. I wondered if Dale Hutchins would fare as well at the hands of the freshman girls.

"That's right, folks, let's make him pay—he gets her for free the other 364 days of the year!" Oz shouted gleefully when a few mischievous buddies decided to give Earl a run for his money. The bidding was hectic for a while—nine, ten-fifty, thirteen—although as my price tag neared twenty, the voices started dying off fast. Earl was just about to bag me for twenty-three fifty when somebody at the rear of the cafeteria abruptly called out twenty-four.

"Twenty-five," Earl said, starting to look a little worried.

"Twenty-five, the man said, a nice round number. I say that's more like it, folks. What do you say we give him a break? Twenty-five once—"

"Thirty."

Some devoted soul trying to jack up the price for the sake of dear old Manahocket? Surely not, I thought, at these rates. I peered back in the direction of the Coke machine, but all the faces seemed to melt into one big blur.

"Thirty-one," Earl called, after a hurried conference with Trisha in which some money appeared to change hands.

"Forty."

Oz looked a little worried too. Earl was one of his dearest friends, yet how did one go about fixing a public auction? "This has to be cash, gents," he stalled. "Cash on the spot."

Earl was appealing frantically to friends standing nearby. "Hold it Oz. Forty-one."

"Forty-one! That's forty-one once, twice, three—"

"Fifty," called out the voice in the rear, clear and confident.

"Fifty," Oz croaked. "Anybody bid fifty-one?"

But nobody was about to bid fifty-one, not even Earl, who was finally out of money and craning his neck indignantly to see what dark horse had dared outbid him on his own girl.

"Sold, to the man in the rear for fifty dollars," Oz sighed.

Voices buzzed, the crowd parted. The winner clumped forward to pay his money and claim his prize. My stomach plunged to the vicinity of my knees as he reached up, seized me lustily around the waist, and swung me to the floor.

"Get a load of these tough-looking legs," Truck Hardy announced to his rowdy band of disciples, and a chorus of sly hoots arose. Earl looked like somebody had just lowered a garage door on his head.

"I'll give you a buzz," my new master said to me, then with no further pleasantries he gathered together his entire lumbering bunch and split the scene.

Perhaps I should take back that earlier remark about Truck Hardy being the biggest hood in the whole school. That wasn't a confirmed fact, just a very strong opinion held by the Albemarle student body in general. The confirmed facts about Truck Hardy were actually pretty scant. He had entered school around the middle of the fall semester, having come from somewhere in the South and/or West. He wore cowboy boots and Levi's and the eternal brown leather jacket, none of them very new. He worked part-time at a gas station near school, and was in all the slow classes with Albemarle's other non-intellectual seniors. He had lost no time after his arrival in acquiring both nickname and reputation in an after-school skirmish that became instant legend. It seems another greaser named Wally Kowalski was spreading shady comments about Hardy's older sister, which Hardy did not at all appreciate. He waited for Wally out in the parking lot to inform him that "I don't take that kind of truck off nobody." He then proceeded to knock Wally flat with one blow, no small feat considering that the unfortunate one made up in girth what he lacked in brain. When Wally's girlfriend, Kate Johnson, immediately put down the loser and took up with the victor, Truck Hardy gained the added reputation of invincible lover.

It wasn't hard to see why, once you took the trouble to give him a good close look. He had the kind of appearance that grows on you, by which I mean that his looks were all tied up somehow with his personality. Medium-tall but really well-built, so that he seemed bigger than he actually was. Hair dark and wavy, not so much long as just heavy. And thick sideburns framing his smooth, absolutely unblemished face, as though he had left behind the adolescent skin scene long ago. His mouth was full and sturdy and could be made to look either lovable or threatening, as the occasion required. That probably would have been his best feature, if it hadn't been for his eyes, which were the real clinchers. Big and lazy and deep-sea green, with lashes long enough to make him look innocent as a choirboy in spite of it all.

Then of course there was the supporting cast, the sort of fellows who never come inside at high school dances, just lurk around the gym entrance transforming a harmless record hop into a truly risky occasion. There were Ray somebody and Mac somebody and even Wally Kowalski, who swiftly recovered his dignity to become Truck's loyal right-hand man. Last but certainly not least was Kate Johnson, gum-chomping queen of the clan, with hair dyed flame-red and teased all over, and eye makeup half an inch thick. Occasional tales would drift around school about her hair-pulling fights with other girls over Truck. In general the whole gang of them resembled a walking soap opera, which we observed with amusement from afar. I say from afar because it was sort of automatically understood that they had their thing and the rest of us non-greaser teens had our thing, and we didn't bother each other. I didn't really feel superior about it—let's just say I didn't expect to sleep any easier being the object of Truck Hardy's attention or Kate Johnson's wrath.

As if all this wasn't enough for my nervous system to cope with, Earl's great good-naturedness suddenly evaporated when it was needed most. Because no male had ever publicly challenged his claim on me, I had no way of knowing about this latent little jealous streak he seemed to have.

Why did Truck Hardy choose me, out of all the slaves he could have picked?

What was that remark about my legs? I must have been flirting with him on the sly or something.

If I wanted to date this hood, why didn't I come out and say so? We had a free and open relationship, we didn't need to sneak around about things, right?

Trisha helped a lot too, whispering things like, "Oh, he is yummy, isn't he? Just catch the way he looks at you, please," whenever Truck passed us in the halls. I, of course, was not catching any such thing. I was looking intensely at my feet, trying to figure a way to get out of it.

"I could pretend I was sick or something on Slave Day. My mother would probably write me a note."

"What are you worried about? It says in the bylaws you can't make your slave do anything illegal."

"I wonder if he's read a copy of the bylaws."

"He did pay fifty dollars for you, don't forget. Which will send practically a whole kid to camp. Ethically speaking—"

And it was only for one day, after all. In broad daylight, in a public school building with about fifteen hundred other people all around. So I decided to think positively. Even when he waited to give me a buzz until the night before Slave Day at eleven-thirty, which is not exactly my mother's concept of the ideal time for phone calls. Even when I could hear what sounded like thirty-five guys in the background laughing and shouting out suggestions, many of them not quite printable.

Sure enough, I was destined to be a slave with many masters. The next morning a great threatening horde of greasers descended upon me bearing gifts. A slightly soiled service-station cap. A grass skirt. A sweat shirt advertising "fast, dependable" spark plugs. A toy wagon. A shoulder-strap signboard with "Hardy's Truck Stop, 24-hour Service" on one side and "If You Don't See It, Ask For It" on the other.

"Try out the ting-a-ling," Wally urged, ringing the bicycle bell attached to the sign. An amused crowd of early-bus arrivals with nothing better to do had gathered to watch. "I mean, man, you gotta ring your ting-a-ling so everybody'll get out of the way of your little red wagon." The idea was, Ray explained, that I would carry their books for them all in the wagon between classes. Truck just stood to one side smoking a Lucky Strike, like a big daddy watching his kids play with a new toy.

Safety in numbers, I kept telling myself as I trooped around the halls pulling the wagon, wearing the sign, ringing the bell. "Yoo-hoo," sang out a wispy falsetto. It turned out to be Mick Morton in a bra and miniskirt, scrubbing the school crest with a toothbrush. I tipped my cap and rang my bell. It could've been a lot worse, actually.

"Meet us right here as soon as the period's over," Wally instructed at the door of their first-hour class, Miss Strickland's DD English Section. DD for Dumb-Dumb. Composed of all the seniors considered least likely to have a burning interest in English literature.

"Don't be late," Ray added.

As for Truck, he had already gone in and taken a seat behind Kate Johnson, who was slumped petulantly in her seat looking ready to make his life miserable in countless ways. What was he trying to prove? Why did he pay fifty dollars for me just to let his friends run the whole show? What did Kate Johnson have that I didn't have, as if I didn't know? Not complaining, of course, just wondering.

At lunchtime his only request was that I bring him three doughnuts, which he didn't eat. He sat thumbing through a hot-rod magazine quietly ignoring Kate Johnson, who was boisterously ignoring him about three tables over. Meanwhile his friends sent me running all over the cafeteria to bring them this, bring them that, take their trays back when they were done. I was just about to beg five minutes for a rest break when Truck suddenly stood up, asked the rest of them to "can it," and beckoned me outside. I couldn't decide whether to cringe or cheer.

It was a perfect April day, pale-green leaves just budding out and bright white clouds like funny monster-shapes all over the sky.

"You about ready to get down to work?" he said.

I considered that a pretty loaded question, but replied that he was the master, I merely the slave.

"I just now figured out what to do with you. My car needs a good wash and wax job. If we start now and you work fast and don't mess around we got just about enough time before I have to go to work this afternoon."

"You mean, leave school?" I said warily. "Like, right now?"

His eyes scanned trees, clouds, telephone wires, and finally looked squarely into mine, a mocking sea-green challenge. "Why not? That against your principles or something?"

I hated for him to think I was a big Snow White, scared to skip school, because that really wasn't the point. All I'd be skipping was Music Appreciation, study hall, and a trig class where the teacher never noticed whether the students were there or not anyway. But as for getting in that particular car with this particular guy and taking off into the unknown . . .

"Or is it you still think I bite?"

"Neither one, it's just—I think we better stay here."

"Who's we? You can stay here if you want, I'm going to go wash and wax my car. No way I'm going to sit in classes any more on a day like this. Come on, I'll sign your title over to Wally for the rest of the time."

I really couldn't figure him out at all. "You mean you're going to walk off right in the middle of Slave Day and leave your own slave? Your own fifty-dollar slave?"

"Wouldn't be the first time I put my money on a bad bet. Had you figured for a little better sport, that's all. Come on." He was holding the door for me but I just stood there, torn between these two not-so-great alternatives, going with him or staying with the gorilla gang.

"All right," I said finally as the bell rang. "Let me just sneak in and get my books."

"Books? On Friday?"

And that is how I came to spend the first book-free weekend of my entire school career.

There was a hose hookup and stuff at the apartment where he lived, he said as we roared away from Albemarle. I may have forgotten to mention that he had a slight Southern and/or Western accent. Nothing too soupy, just the faintest hint of a drawl. Pastel visions of cactus against the sunset, live oaks dripping with Spanish moss.

"Smoke?" He offered me a Lucky Strike, which I declined. He lit himself one, using both hands despite the fact that he's doing about fifty-five in a thirty zone. Along about then I began groping for a seat belt, but the floorboards yielded only Dr. Pepper bottles, popcorn boxes, and beer cans.

"How about that other stuff, you smoke that?"

I said no, not really, how about him?

"Nope."

When he'd driven some distance without elaborating on this point, or indeed showing any further signs of conversation at all, I finally inquired about the white plastic figure dangling from the rearview mirror.

"That? Oh, that's my guardian angel. Keeps me and Tortoise out of trouble. We get in some little trouble now and then, but no real big trouble."

"You and *who?*"

"Tortoise. That's my car."

"As in the Tortoise and the Hare?"

"Right. Looks like a sleeper but always wins in the end."

It was, he explained patiently, as if anyone else in the world would automatically know this, a '57 Chevy with a something kind of engine, "dual quads," a something exhaust, and a lot more.

"Boy, that's unbelievable," I said. And to top all this off, he added that next weekend he planned to get him a different kind of "hot cam." I didn't know if this was something you ate or attached to your axle or what, so I just pretended the very thought of it left me speechless.

All this time the radio was blasting forth some truly remarkable country-and-western sounds, including that old favorite, "Mayeek the Wurrrrrld Go Away." Country Carl Barton, the syrupy-tongued D.J., kept saying things like, "Ah'll be back in jist a little while, honey chile, so don't yew touch that dial."

After a few minutes of this I confessed that I had never quite learned to appreciate that type of music.

He shrugged. "It just says what it has to say, plain and simple. Some of it's corny, but some of it's pretty, too, if you really listen to the words."

And so I had my Music Appreciation after all that day, since he graciously left the radio on for me the entire time I scrubbed, rinsed, dusted out, waxed, and shined Tortoise in the back parking lot of a high rise called Lake Pleasant Towers.

"Now this here is a bucket," he said, "and this is a sponge, and you dip this one in that one, but first you got to go over there and draw you up some water."

"Very funny."

"And just to make sure you don't get lazy and start skipping over places, I'm going to stand right here."

I thought it was pushing it a bit to say Tortoise needed washing. It appeared Truck spent the greater part of his days keeping his car groomed and ready for whatever might come along. But I wasn't complaining any. In fact it felt kind of kicky and free, slopping around in all that water listening to hillbilly music on such a magnificent spring day. Even with Truck Hardy standing right there, managing to squash very neatly any little conversation that might rear its timid head.

"If—"

"You know—"

"Go ahead."

"No, I'm sorry, you go on."

"Nothing important."

"Well, what I was going to say was, I'm kind of an old hand at car washing, since I had to wash about thirty cars during our Trojanette service project last fall."

"Man, you just go around all day doing good deeds, don't you?"

I smiled sweetly and that ended that conversation. What I really wanted to ask him was why on earth he had bought me in the first place, but that seemed a little too personal. So, spotting a scroungy paperback copy of *Romeo and Juliet* on the back seat, I asked him if he was reading *Romeo and Juliet*.

"Nope."

"Already finished it?"

"Nope."

I began making it into a sort of game. Like the way I played tennis—just get the ball back over the net, never mind your style.

"Haven't started it yet?"

"Yeah. I started it. But after three pages I couldn't figure out one thing they were talking about so I said the hell with it. Guess I'm just dumb or something. I'm in all the dumb classes, that must make me dumb." Slight pause. "Right?"

Well, it was progress. Somewhere underneath that tough-guy routine he was waiting to hear what I thought of him.

"Sure, you're dumb all right. About as dumb as a fox."

Out of eight thousand possible answers, I believe I hit on just the one he wanted to hear.

"I mean, I know you're supposed to love Shakespeare and all that, but if he's going to say something seems like he could come right out and say it, instead of going around in circles with all that symbolism and stuff."

"That's just the way they wrote back then. You have to read the footnotes."

"Oh, sure. You read a line and then you have to look down at the notes to see what you just read. See page twenty-six, it says. So you look it up on page twenty-six and you think, man, is that all he's trying to say? Then you go back to where you were, except you can't find your place, so you got to start over, and pretty soon you're lost again so you look and there's this note that says, see page forty-eight. Yeah, you bet, those footnotes are a big help. Who needs it? Anyway, I saw the movie."

"But that's not the same as reading and studying a work of literature, just sitting watching a movie."

"What are you, in training to be some kind of English teacher or something?"

"Yeah," I said defensively. "Maybe so, some day."

He shot me a heavy glance. "Of all the things to want to be. An English teacher. Man, I know when I die and go down to the hot place, the one with the pitchfork's gonna turn out to be some old-maid English teacher. Let me just tell you the kind of luck I have in English." I have always been suspicious of people who speak of classwork in terms of luck, but I let him tell me anyway.

"Miss Pettigrew, this teacher's name was. Eighth grade. She was teaching us this thing on outside reading, 'The Wonderful Wide World of Books' or something dumb like that, but I gotta say, for once in my life I did have me a book I could get past the first page on. Only book I ever read all the way through to the end, every page, instead of just skipping around looking for the easy parts."

"What was it, for pity's sake?"

"The Old Man and the Sea."

Not a bad choice, I thought, for somebody who'd read only one book.

"I mean, the guy that wrote it, what's-his-name—"

"Hemingway."

"Yeah, him. You talk about a writer just coming right out and telling the story, period, without a bunch of fancy bull, just damn saying what he means."

"I know," I said. I only happened to be the biggest Hemingway fan in the greater metropolitan area.

"So anyway, we were supposed to do a book report, five hundred words, about the characters and the set-ting and the plot and all that junk. I was really charged up about this book, except every time I started writing something down it sounded stupid, like I was just saying the same thing the writer did only not near as good as he already said it. So I didn't hand in a report. The teacher made me stay after school and gave me this big lecture about not handing in assignments. I told her I read the book, why did I have to write anything about reading the book? She said because everybody else in the class had to write a book report, and how come I thought I was so special? And besides, if I didn't write this report, how would she know if I really read it? I said I read it all right, in fact I liked it so much I even went back and read some parts over again, because I liked to fish myself and I could tell this guy knew what he was talking about, catching fish and all. I told her I gave her my word. She said that's fine, honey, now all you need is 499 more. She was always calling everybody 'honey,' Pettigrew was. I couldn't stand that."

"So what did you do?"

"Oh, I finally wrote up something just to hand in. Which she gave back with all these notes about words misspelled and 'this is not a complete sentence,' plus two grades off for being two days late, so you flunk, honey. That's what I mean about my luck in English, I get an F for reading the only goddamn book I ever really read. What do you think I'm in all the dumb classes for?"

In this and other frustrating ways, the afternoon passed.

During the breathing spell between washing and waxing, Truck said he was going to run upstairs for a minute to get something cold to drink. "You been a pretty good slave, I might even bring you one down."

"Couldn't I come with you, please?"

"Look, you don't want to go up there, the place is a mess."

"I don't care how messy it is, if it's got a ladies' room."

"Oh." I think he actually blushed. "Yeah, O.K."

On the way around the building there was a splendid view of Lake Pleasant itself, a bad joke from any angle. It was a mudhole, with a broken-down dock and debris floating in the stagnant water around the edges.

"I can't get over these mothers calling that a lake," he said disgustedly. "Where I come from, that's known as a cesspool."

"Where do you come from?"

"Man, you name it. One thing we never could seem to do, and that is stay around any place long enough to get ourselves in the phone book."

He had come from West Virginia most recently, he finally told me. Before that, a couple of places in Tennessee. "Lakes so big and wide you can fish them for hours and never see shore on the other side. Look down out of the boat and see the bluegill and bass coming right up to the top of the water, looking for bait, show me the hook, man, watch me chomp it."

"What does your father do?"

He drew a long sigh. "I don't know what he does now, but I can tell you what he used to do. He used to drink and gamble and run around with good-looking women. Last seen about six years ago, headed toward Alaska to make a killing in the oil fields. Anything else you want to know?"

"I'm sorry," I said sheepishly.

"Yeah, me too. Next time remind me to get me a slave that's not quite so nosy." Healthy curiosity, my teachers always called it.

Lake Pleasant Towers was not much better inside than out, with fake plants, fake wood, even a couple of fake chandeliers in the lobby. Upstairs it smelled like a giant cooking contest was in progress, Mexican food on one side of the hall and Italian on the other. When he opened the door to their apartment I could see right away why he hadn't been too eager to show it off. It looked as though they were either just moving in or just moving out. I thought how my mother would have fainted at the sight of the junk scattered all over, no curtains on the windows, no paintings on the walls.

Mary Lynn, the legendary sister, was lounging on the sofa watching a soap opera on TV and eating small, gnarled doughnuts. She was pretty in a limp sort of way, with blonde hair that was probably not authentic, I sensed even in the dim light. Mary Lynn worked the early shift at the doughnut shop, Truck informed me. His old lady worked the late shift at the telephone company. That way somebody was always there to look after Davey.

Davey, I must admit, came as a real surprise. He looked about three or four and was beautiful, a miniature Truck Hardy, big soft eyes and shaggy hair and everything. At the sound of Truck's voice he came tearing out of a bedroom and flung himself around Truck's legs, crying, "Bubba! Bubba!" Truck was mortified, no doubt about it.

"Bubba?" I said.

Fortunately a commercial came on just then, or we might never have heard from Mary Lynn. She gave me a quick sizing-up, gestured at Truck, and said, "His real name's Lamar."

"Lamar!"

Truck gave her a very unfriendly look.

"Lamar Puckett Hardy," she went on, grinning broadly between doughnuts.

"Lamar," I murmured.

"That's just between you and me, understand? They don't know anything but L. P. at school."

Mary Lynn showed further signs of hospitality by offering me a doughnut. They were rejects, she explained, mangled in one way or another by the doughnut machine. "They taste O.K., they just look funny. They give us all we want to take home."

So as not to hurt her feelings I accepted a doughnut, at which point the soap opera resumed and the conversation abruptly ended. Truck pointed out the bathroom without quite looking at me. I made a quick, discreet trip, drank half a Coke and was ready to go again.

"Take Davey!" Mary Lynn bellowed when we were halfway to the elevator. Davey was all for this, too, so we didn't have much choice. Mary Lynn was divorced, Truck said bluntly by way of explanation. Married at sixteen, divorced at seventeen, with Davey arriving somewhere in between.

"She didn't know which end was up but she found out quick enough when that big hunk left her holding the bag. Worst part is, now she'll do headstands for any guy who'll date her more than twice in a row. She's not exactly a front runner any more."

At that depressing thought, the elevator doors lurched open and Davey bolted for the parking lot.

Car-waxing turned out to be a real challenge that afternoon. I was tired, and although Davey was adorable, he was also very much underfoot. I tried my best schoolteacher psychology on him, but I wasn't making much progress. He kept picking up pebbles and putting them in the wax can, helpful things like that.

Truck wasn't much solace either, having retired to supervise from the shade of a nearby tree. "Man, you are some lucky slave," he reminded me from time to time. "Ain't every master lets his slave have a real live assistant."

Finally I devised the clever plan of letting Davey draw pictures in the film of dried wax before I rubbed it off. He was extremely creative, I'll say that for him. He drew a total of forty-six monsters on the left-hand door alone, and told me the life history of every one of them.

It was a blessed moment when the master called out time to quit. He was due at work in a couple of minutes and would have to take me home, even though I hadn't finished waxing the left rear fender.

"Well, Teach," he said on the way, "what's the lucky college going to get you this fall?"

Gloom. Had I actually managed to forget about it for a whole afternoon? I told him about my sad status at the place I really wanted to go, probably having to settle for this other place that was far less impressive, being so terribly disappointed. He completely failed to see the pathos of it.

"So big deal. At least you're going somewhere they got soft beds and decent food and a big library you can sit around in all day and read Shakespeare, if that's what you want to do. I mean, you take me now, only waiting list I'm on is Uncle Sam's. Closest I'll ever get to a college campus is if they send in the troops to put down a riot."

Unfortunately we had just pulled into my driveway when this meaty subject of war and peace arose, a topic I really would have liked to hear his thoughts on. Except I could see at a glance I was in big trouble already, since Earl's VW was parked out front.

"Well, I hope I was worth fifty dollars."

"I'd say about forty-nine fifty, without that rear fender."

"Okay, so I owe you a rear fender."

"Money's just money," he shrugged. "Anyway, it went for a good cause. You figure, some of those city kids are going to find out for the first time what a real lake looks like."

Noble creature! I felt I owed him at least a rear fender.

"Listen, I really mean it. A deal's a deal. I'll finish up what I didn't get done. You just bring me that can of wax, let me know when."

He smiled. Considering it was his first smile of the day, it was like a major event. "O.K., how about Saturday night?" He wasn't kidding, either. I uh-ed and well-ed and finally came out with some pretty uptight-sounding stuff to the effect that we had better make it some afternoon instead, since I was sort of more or less going with somebody.

"Yeah, come to think of it, I am too." He then gunned his engine a few times, told me to "be good," and proceeded to break all previous speed records for backing out of our driveway.

All of which Earl had obviously been watching from the window.

"That was illegal, leaving school in the middle of the day. You realize that, don't you? It's none of my business of course. If you wanted to run off and marry the guy I wouldn't stop you. But it happens to state clearly in the bylaws that you can't make your slave do something illegal." He had apparently been at my house since three-thirty that afternoon keeping a nervous vigil with my mother, who could not seem to get it through her head that I would do something illegal.

"He didn't make me," I said. "I consented."

"Oh. *Well.* Why didn't you say so?"

Chapter 3

I suppose if I had been a little more repentant, or Earl a little more forgiving, Slave Day would have been shrugged off and forgotten and I might even have ended up Mrs. Earl Corbett today. However, as I already mentioned, he had this jealousy problem that would have put Othello to shame. On our date that very night, with a Shell credit card and practically a full tank of gas, he drove six blocks out of his way and pulled into a Texaco station. Right away I figured he was up to no good.

"What are you doing?"

"What do you think?" he said innocently.

I thought it was just our luck, with two other guys on duty, that it was my ex-master who came ambling over in his gray-striped uniform with "L. P. Hardy" embroidered on the pocket. I also remember having the distinct thought that a sexy-looking guy could look sexy wearing almost anything.

"Give me fifty dollars worth of regular," Earl said. Truck gave us a funny look, first Earl and then me, like he was wondering whether to laugh or what.

"Fifty dollars?"

"Oh, sorry, did I say fifty dollars? No, no, I meant fifty *cents* worth. And would you check the oil and clean off the windshield while you're at it?"

I didn't know what he was trying to prove, but it was quite a scene. Earl humming along with the radio, trying to hide the fact that he is watching me closely for my reaction. Me looking around at all the little gas station flags, trying to hide the fact that I am watching Truck closely for his reaction. Truck pumping gas and checking the oil and washing the windshield, trying to catch my eye with looks like, *You aren't really going with this lunchbox, are you, baby?*

Actually, washing the windshield is putting it mildly. Not only did he scrape in slow strokes to get off all the bug spots, he also came around and wiped the windows on my side, then around to the rear oval window, and those on the other side. Just generally giving us A-1 service, whistling while he worked.

"How about a little air in your tires?"

"No thanks, that's all."

"You sure? It's free."

"No, that's all right." Earl thrust him a handful of pennies, another feature of this hilarious prank, and started to put the car in gear.

"Wait a minute, I'll get your stamps."

Now, Earl had been saving stamps for months and months to get a high-intensity lamp for college, and he never passed up a stamp. He gave me a very exasperated smile as Truck clumped back into the station, taking his sweet time.

"Here you go." He handed Earl the five stamps. Then with his dirty, rough hand, grease caked underneath the nails and a Band-Aid around his thumb, he reached across Earl and gave me a big red lollipop. "And a sucker for the little gal."

This was my idea of a pretty brilliant putdown, especially considering it was completely off-the-cuff, but I must admit it didn't do much to improve Earl's mood that evening.

"I think what you should do is date this guy a couple of times," he kept saying. "Actually, it would be a very good experience for you. Very educational."

"I don't want to date this guy," I insisted, which seemed to make no difference.

"He's obviously interested in you, probably just hesitates to make his move because of me. His friend Cunningham is in my homeroom, it should be an easy matter to let him know you're free to date whoever you want to, whenever you want to—"

I informed him in a semi-shriek that, for the record, Truck Hardy had not hesitated at all to ask me out and I had turned him down flat. I thought this would be reasonable proof that I was not interested in Truck Hardy, but for some strange reason it had the opposite effect.

"To tell you the truth, Jean, there are a few people I'd like to date myself, so this really might be a good thing. I mean, we've always had a very mature agreement about dating, right? No need to get all emotional about it."

The first of these "few people" turned out to be Trisha Sewall, which was *not* my idea of a brilliant putdown. In fact, I considered it strictly seventh-grade stuff to try to make one jealous by dating one's best friend. And dating her four nights in a row, during track season yet. And taking her to large Albemarle gatherings so the maximum number of people would see them. The shock of it was what hurt the most, I think—that somebody like Earl Corbett would sink into such hysterics over something so petty.

I knew exactly what he was up to, since he continued to call me about three times a day to assure me that we were both mature people and still excellent friends.

And, he always vaguely implied, we might even get back together some day when I had learned whatever lesson all this was supposed to be teaching me.

"There's no reason why we can't still have fun together," he said during one of these calls. "All three of us, Trisha too. No need to get emotional with Trisha about it."

Actually, I had never considered getting emotional with Trisha about it. Trisha Sewall had about as much malice in her soul as Stanley, and I couldn't blame her for a thing. Especially since she called me up herself about three times a day to make sure I didn't hate her. I think she saw herself as a character in a great drama, with fate pulling the strings, and I didn't begrudge her the role.

The one who did get all emotional about it was my mother. How could I have gone and blown it like that, her bewildered expression demanded, when I had this fabulous fellow practically in the bag? She kept making helpful suggestions like, why didn't I give a little party? Why didn't I get my hair cut and restyled and buy a new spring outfit?

Then of course there was Truck Hardy, the most maddening figure of all, cruising around Albemarle like Robin Hood with his lusty wench and his band of merry men—totally oblivious to the shambles he had managed to make of my private life.

After I had spent a week of long evenings holed up in my room with Stanley and my Princess phone, alternating between feelings of fury and despair, my father came up with a suggestion I almost liked.

"Why don't you take that bus trip down to Darcey over the weekend? After all, you've never even laid eyes on the place."

True, I thought, very true. And it would also get me out of town for two days, which seemed like a great idea in itself.

Needless to say, I didn't go down there expecting a whole lot. Not much more, in the words of L. P. Hardy, than a place that had soft beds and decent food and a library where you could sit around and read Shakespeare all day.

The way it worked out was this: the beds and food were O.K., but the library was still under construction—pale pink, naked-looking brick, anemic little trees, big mounds of mud.

"The new building will house all the media," Dr. Bradley explained proudly, taking me on a personal campus tour. "Films, tapes, microfilms, language labs, screening rooms—the works. We've been using the manor house up till now, but it's really been a pinch."

"The manor house?"

"Yes, from the old plantation itself. All this used to be a big estate—you knew that, didn't you? We're using the original buildings wherever feasible, for the time being. The barn, for instance, houses the art department. And we renovated the stables for the education department." I squinted intently at the long, narrow building he pointed out across the lawn. That's what it looked like, sure enough, an old renovated plantation stable.

"There's our latest addition, the Student Union," he concluded, indicating a weird combination of molded stucco and black glass in the distance. "As you can see, our architecture is sort of Modern Eclectic."

I thought Modern Mess was more like it. I nearly wept to think of my idyllic visit to Holyoke back in the fall—lovely red and gold leaves scattered along rustic walks, ivy curling up stately stone towers, mossy statues of campus saints.

Darcey also looked slightly deserted. "Saturday afternoon," Dr. Bradley commented. "Everybody wants to be somewhere else, you know how it is. There's some kind of rock concert down by the lake, maybe Sara Jo Ferguson will take you down there."

Sara Jo Ferguson was my hostess for the weekend. She was a senior zoology major who looked like the coed least likely to attend a rock concert or have a date on Saturday night, but she did turn out to be pretty nice. At least she lived in the coed dorm my father was always talking about, which meant there were a bunch of other dateless types, both male and female, playing records and forming up bridge games and doing their laundry together.

I wandered around behind Sara Jo all evening getting shown different spots and introduced to different people until ten-thirty, when Sara Jo suddenly remembered something she'd forgotten to do to her fruit flies and swiftly departed for the zoology lab. This left me stranded in the snack kitchen with a guy named Jonathan, who had just put a batch of brownies in the oven and was waiting for them to bake. He was also smoking marijuana like mad, leaning over the sink letting the ashes go down the garbage disposal. He said that it was always best to smoke in the kitchen or bathroom or near a window, that way you could dispose of the evidence at a second's notice. He then went on to tell me, in great loving detail, how he had narrowly escaped getting busted in Buffalo one time, and how he had just missed being picked up at the Washington National Airport, all of which made me wish I'd gone to look at the fruit flies.

He was in the middle of some classic tale about outwitting customs agents at the Canadian border when somewhere down the hall somebody put on Simon and Garfunkel's old "Bridge Over Troubled Water" album and turned it up loud. At the very first of those calm, majestic piano chords I thought about Ben, how "Bridge" was his all-time favorite album, and a sudden awful wave of homesickness or loneliness or something washed over me, right there in the snack kitchen, some depressing blend of Darcey and Earl and Trisha all mixed up with that sickly-sweet smoke, and I had a desperate urge to call up Ben and talk things over. Just go right down the hall to the pay phone and call him up, I thought. Why not?

Yale was a pretty long way from Darcey, so I charged it to our home phone. It rang at his dorm in New Haven about eighty-five times and finally some guy answered it and said he wasn't there, but he could maybe be reached at this other number. So the operator tried that and it rang there about eighty-five more times and some girl answered and by the time Ben's voice finally said "Hello?" I felt kind of dumb and baby-sisterish about the whole thing.

"Hi," I said. "How've you been?"

"Well, I'm still alive." Just barely, it appeared, from the sound of his voice. "Are the folks O.K.? Anything wrong?"

"Not really, I just—needed cheering up a little, and I figured you were the one for the job."

"No, no," I heard him say to somebody in the background. "It's Sheena, Queen of the Jungle. She needs cheering up, was that a stroke of genius? To call on me when she needs cheering up? So. What's the trouble?"

"Well, to begin with, Holyoke put me on their waiting list, and my boyfriend ran off with my best friend, all in the same week."

"Trisha? Sewall? With old Superjock? Hell, I think that's pretty cheerful right there! What did you say the other one was?"

"Mount Holyoke. You know, where I've been counting on going since I was three years old. They put me on their waiting list, and you know what that means. Right now I'm calling you from Darcey College—that's where I am this weekend. It's awful, down in the middle of nowhere. Chances are ninety-to-one this is where I'll end up." I continued on in this vein for about three dollars worth of Bell Telephone time.

"I hardly know what to tell you, Sheena," Ben said

when I finally rested my case. "Except maybe, 'They also serve who only stand and wait.' Quote, John Milton, *On His Blindness*."

"Boy, that's terrific, you got any more?"

"Yeah, here's one—more recent words of wisdom from the British Isles. 'You can't always get what you want.' Quote, The Rolling Stones, *Let It Bleed*."

"Whose side are you on, anyway?"

"Hey, look. I hate to be a drag about this, but did you ever try counting your blessings? I mean, there's people dying out there for God's sake, nineteen-year-old soldiers with peach fuzz on their cheeks getting their legs blown off in Cong booby traps because they couldn't afford the price of a student deferment, to *any* college, and you're bawling because you got put on the waiting list of one school and only got accepted by about four others—I mean, you're my sister and I love you, Jeannie, but get your head straight, you know what I mean?"

"O.K.," I said contritely. "I know what you mean. I'm sorry."

"Because look, I don't care how bad it is, you can find something you like about anything sooner or later, if you give it a chance. Like, in the long run it doesn't really matter where the hell you go, it's what you do when you get there that counts. People have even been known to flunk out of Yale on occasion, you realize that? I may even illustrate that principle myself shortly."

"Is that why you didn't come home spring vacation?"

"Wait a minute now, Sheena. We're talking about you. Spring vacation, man, that's another story. Like I told the folks sixty times, I just felt like taking a little trip with my roommate."

"You're going to be home in time for my graduation, aren't you?"

"You bet I am. In fact, I'm going to bring the entire Yale Glee Club and we'll sing the Whiffenpoof Song when they call out your name for the diploma. Jeannette

Gordon Travis, baaa, baaa, baaaaa. Now, you feel all better?"

"Yes," I said, and after I told him so long and hung up and went back to Sara Jo's room, I really did feel better. Darcey certainly hadn't changed any, I guess my head had just moved a couple of degrees in the right direction. Ben could do it all right, one way or another.

I kept thinking about what he had said all during the long ride home the next day. The bus was full of young soldiers, with that look on their faces like they've just been somewhere and they're headed somewhere else, and I could not get the horrible image out of my mind of nineteen-year-old kid soldiers with peach fuzz on their cheeks getting their legs blown off in Cong booby traps because they couldn't afford the price of a student deferment. What was it Truck Hardy had said? *Only waiting list I'm on is Uncle Sam's.* Sorry, sugar, no sympathy at all. Ben's sentiments exactly, as a matter of fact. Just slightly different phrasing. That seemed strange, since I couldn't imagine two more opposite characters than Ben Travis and Truck Hardy.

And Superjock. I thought about him, too, but with a different feeling. Somehow, sitting on that bus watching the spring-green Virginia countryside sail by, the whole Earl Corbett issue seemed terribly silly. Especially considered that my unfaithfulness consisted exclusively of a car wash and a red sucker and an occasional "Hi ya, Teach" while passing in the halls. I wondered if my old master was really all that unaware of the fireworks he had touched off. In any case, it was bound to filter down to him sooner or later, the way gossip traveled around that school. And then what?

"Beg pardon, Miss," said the boy next to me, a broad-shouldered Marine with eyes a little bit like guess who. "But ah wonder if it would bothah yew too much if ah smoked?" Lucky Strikes, of course. In the end I simply reclined my seat and closed my eyes and indulged in some long, confused thoughts about Truck Hardy.

I've never been much of a believer in ESP, but there lay that incredible note on the phone pad when I got back home that Sunday afternoon: "Boy called."

"What boy?" I asked my mother, with my heart lodged uneasily in the pit of my stomach.

"Oh, some boy," she said. "I kept asking him may I tell her who called please, but he didn't seem to get the hint. Didn't leave a message, just said he would call back."

Chapter 4

My first date with Truck Hardy has to have been one of the more colorful first dates in the history of organized courtship. Not since the days of cavemen dragging off girls by the hair, I'm sure, have any parents been so perplexed by what came to pick up their daughter. I tried to prepare them in advance by explaining that he was a more simple and down-to-earth boy than most of my friends, and really hard-working, since he held down a part-time job besides going to school. However, there seemed to be no classy synonyms for "gas station," and I think all my careful preparation only set them up to expect the worst. When eight-thirty came they were both posted coincidentally in the living room, my father watching some silly TV show and my mother dusting off furniture for the seventeenth time that day. This made me so nervous that I went upstairs to comb my hair and go to the bathroom again, during which time he arrived.

From my bedroom window I spotted him ambling up our long flagstone walk. He had on a bright red shirt and some sort of pants I presumed to be what cowboys wear whenever they aren't rounding up cattle.

He also had on his boots. I must point out that although Albemarle High School had gone through a brief cowboy-boot fad back around Christmas, Truck Hardy wore boots before the fad began and continued to wear them after it had passed. Completing this outfit was a black-and-white cowhide vest he had been substituting for the brown leather jacket now that the weather was warmer. I don't mean the kind of suede-trimmed fake-fur vest you'd pay sixty-five dollars for at Lord and Taylor's; I mean it was obvious that this cowhide had once been on the side of a cow. Frankly I thought it was the coolest thing I'd ever seen, but I was afraid my parents wouldn't be quite so impressed.

I took a deep breath and hurried downstairs to save him from certain destruction, only to find him holding his own quite well with Ed and Edith in the foyer. He was admiring an antique cabinet they took great pride in, discussing the style and date, grain of wood, and type of finish. He must have been getting it all right, too, from the looks on their faces.

"What have you been doing, reading up on antiques?" I said as he ushered me into Tortoise and drove away at a respectable speed.

"Just like a teach. You think everything's gotta come out of books."

"Don't tell me, let me guess. You're really a New England antique dealer in disguise."

"Try West Virginia."

When he was a kid, he said, he had done odd jobs for a dealer. "This guy would go around and buy stuff like, say, a solid cherry chest of drawers, two hundred years old, from some old farmer. Pay him fifteen dollars for it. Then he'd pay me a couple of bucks to refinish it, sand it down, and rub it with linseed oil. Then he'd sell it for seventy-five to some Yankee picker traveling the circuit, who would probably turn around and sell it to a fancy city shop for a hundred and fifty, where some old rich lady would buy it for three hundred. How's that for inflation?"

"Sounds more like a racket to me." I never had been what you'd call a connoisseur of antiques.

"Oh, I don't know. Look at it this way, that chest came out of a fifteen-dollar corner of that old farmer's attic and went into a three-hundred-dollar corner of the rich lady's pad."

That, I had to admit, was an interesting way of looking at it.

"There's a good living in it, if you know what you're doing. Like anything else, you find a lot of real artists and a lot of real crooks. Just depends what you're in it for."

I found this rather encouraging when I thought about it a minute, this prospect of finding a respectable little niche for him in the capitalist system. "You think maybe you'll end up doing something in that line? Be an antique dealer or something?"

"No, Teach, I think I'm just gonna pump gas all my life."

About that time we arrived at the movies, a local drive-in known better as the Passion Pit. When I saw *Hellcat Queen* and *Blood Lust of Dracula* up on the marquee I figured I was in for a real grade-D evening, but I was wrong again.

Entertainment at the Pit, you see, had nothing to do with the movies. The Tortoise actually became a sort of cocktail lounge on wheels. As soon as we arrived, people started popping in, friends roaming from car to car to bum cigarettes and beer and exchange the latest gossip. Kate Johnson, by her own account, had supposedly put down Truck for good and was already practically engaged to a sailor.

"You hear that?" Truck said, dropping a few comic sobs upon my shoulder. "Looks like I'm all yours."

I seemed to be an object of much curiosity, as if everyone just had to stop by to see what a clean-living intellectual like me had that Kate Johnson didn't have. I kept getting greetings like Wally's: "Say, Brainy, think you could explain *Huck Finn* to me? We gotta read it and I don't understand it."

"Huck Finn can't figure you out either," Truck told him drily, whereupon the conversation switched to some "mean mothers from Sutton" that Mac had seen parked over on the other side of the Snack Bar, and what to do about it. Truck advised just forgetting it. They all looked from him to me and back to him with great suspicion, like I had put him under some kind of peace-mongering spell or something.

All this time, guys kept squeezing in and out of Tortoise, some stag and some with dates. At one point there were fully ten souls crammed together drinking and jesting and delivering critical comments on *Hellcat Queen,* whose heroine made Kate Johnson look like Princess Grace.

One unsettling side effect of these crowded conditions was that I was forced to sit very close to Truck, in his lap at times, so that I gradually developed a philosophical theory about drive-in movies. My theory is, that if you are at a drive-in movie sitting in the lap of a boy who is eating popcorn, drinking Bud, smelling faintly of English Leather, keeping track of all his friends' conversations, glancing at the screen occasionally, and all this while still managing to hold your hand and rub his thumb in a slow circle across your palm, I say, my theory is that even if this guy looks like the Hunchback of Notre Dame, you are bound to start wondering sooner or later what it would be like should he decide to lean over a few more inches and kiss you.

Nothing seemed likely right then, with his friends packed cozily all around, but it was only a matter of time until they began departing in twos and threes. By the time intermission was over and the lights went down for *Blood Lust of Dracula,* Tortoise was dark, private, and spacious once again, and filled with nervous vibrations. Hormones are funny like that.

Well, not really all that funny.

I mean, I think sex is a completely natural and wholesome God-given human function. I just wonder why God couldn't have waited to give this particular function a bit later in the human cycle, instead of throwing it in during adolescence before you're old enough to be married, old enough to be finished with your education, and in most states, before you're even old enough to drive. Like, one day you're out riding bikes with your friends and the next day *zap*, a whole new world is unloaded onto your innocent shoulders—a fun-filled world of teenform bras, naughty dreams, romantic traumas, and heart-to-heart talks with Mother.

My mother never really terrorized me about sex, she merely gave me several stiff doses of the "seduced and abandoned" theory. That is, if you are so wanton and foolish as to allow the first to happen, the second will surely follow. With the probable result that you will emerge emotionally crippled and ruined for enjoyment of sex with your eventual husband (if, indeed, you can subsequently find anyone willing to marry you) for the rest of your life.

And then of course there were the "growing up" films foisted upon us in junior high school. They took a week out of gym class between hockey and badminton and let us have it all at once, beginning with *A New You*, about menstrual periods, followed by *Miracle of Life*, about male and female reproductive systems, and finally a true-life tale entitled *Lost Along the Way*, about illicit teen-age sex. Judging from clothing and hair styles this latter flick was made in about 1945 and was filled with every conceivable statistic, from the mathematic odds on sperm meeting egg to the numbers of illegitimate children born each year broken down into socio-economic classifications. The only thing it did not provide was some glimmering of how, when, and where illicit teen-age sex takes place, not to mention *why*.

For instance, none of those junior-high-school lessons offered any concrete suggestions on how to keep cool when you're alone with a known seducer at the drive-in movies and he sighs comfortably, lounges back against the door, and pulls you down so that you're halfway lying in his lap with his arms folded snugly just beneath your absurdly pounding heart.

In all fairness, I must admit he did make it clear from the outset how much he respected me. He was glad, he said, that I didn't pay any attention to all those stories about him, since the girls involved were a completely different kind. There were plenty of those kind around. It was girls like me that were a vanishing breed, nice girls who wanted to stay nice girls but were still good sports who knew how to have fun. In fact, I was the kind of girl a guy could have a great time with on the first date without even trying to put the make on, even a guy like him.

"Thank you," I said humbly, wondering for a minute if he actually planned to keep this relationship platonic.

A minute was about as long as I had to wonder, however. That's how long it took him to get back into action, this time exploring with gentle fingertips all the little intricacies of my forearm, shoulder, collarbone, and ear lobe.

Devastatingly gentle.

I was just beginning to tune out the hairy vampire up on the screen, who was using roughly the same technique on his sweet young victims, when Wally's fat grinning face suddenly appeared in the window above the loudspeaker.

"Hey, man, sorry if I'm breaking up something here." He didn't look a bit sorry, he looked delighted. I sat up quickly, and Truck just sighed. "Big action, everybody's hot. The word is, Ross Road at midnight."

"Tell 'em to keep their pants on, the strip out at Broom Creek opens next weekend," Truck answered.

"Broom Creek! Aw, man, don't start that legal drag strip routine again! Those guys are nothing but a bunch of farmers out there."

"Yeah, well, so am I."

"Mattingly bet me you'd pussy out. Said you'd rather sit around here and you know what." Wally looked at me accusingly. "I bet him you'd be there before he was."

"You never been known for making smart bets, Wally."

"Aw, look, man," Wally said in an insinuating drawl. "You're not gonna get this chick on the first date, what are you worried about?"

With that Truck blew out a long count-to-ten breath, gave my knee a regretful squeeze, slid behind the steering wheel, and fired up Tortoise. As we crunched out of the parking lot a sizeable portion of the audience followed. My first impulse was to suggest that he take me home before he went wherever it was he and all these other enthusiasts were going, but after just being hailed as the great American sport, it hardly seemed the thing to do.

Ross Road, I soon learned, was one of several alternating sites for late-night street races between the greasers from Albemarle and the greasers from Sutton. It was a brand-new six-lane boulevard built out in the middle of nowhere, which meant some developer no doubt had plans to build thousands of split-levels on both sides within a year or so.

Makeshift start and finish lines had been drawn across the smooth, straight stretch of asphalt and already a few minor runs were under way, with clusters of raunchy types standing around drinking beer and rooting for their favorite cars and drivers. The guys from Sutton were uniformly bigger, meaner, and greasier than our boys, and had uglier cars. Many hot words were being exchanged. Junior Lee Mattingly, a hawk-nosed individual with a smiling snake tatooed prominently on his forearm, was taking on all comers and beating every one. He occasionally sidled over and threw a few inflammatory words in Truck's direction, which Truck returned with quite a bit more wit and style.

"What kind of car is that he's driving?" I asked at one point, just so he wouldn't forget I was standing there.

"Seventy GTO."

"Kind of nice-looking."

"Want me to fix you up with him?"

"I don't mean the guy, I mean the car. Is a '70 GTO as good as Tortoise, or what?"

"Nothing's as good as Tortoise."

As for the races themselves, they were not exactly my kind of fun. Before each run the fans on the perimeter searched for cops and gave the all-clear sign. Then somebody would come down with the start signal and the two contestants would screech and roar down Ross Road, laying rubber and shooting smoke and just generally doing things I never dreamed regular cars would do on a regular road.

"You're not really going to do that, are you?" I said finally.

"Yeah, I was sort of thinking about it."

"I don't think I want you to do that."

"Oh, you don't, huh?"

"No, I think I want you to take me home."

"Sure, I'll take you home. Just as soon as I finish off that tatooed mother out there, I'll take you home."

"I'd really like to go home right now," I said in as firm and sincere a tone as I could muster. *"Please."*

"Please, huh? You want me to please do this, Wally wants me to please do that, Mattingly wants me to please do something else—I just can't make anybody happy tonight, can I?"

"Why don't you do what *you* want?" I said, which really ripped him off.

"Think I will," he said, stomping off to join a group of beer-swigging cronies, informing me over his shoulder that he would see me around.

Then it was my turn to be ripped off. Without my purse or anything, I took off in the direction of civilization, too furious to be fully aware of the risks I was running. Hairy characters leered at me as I passed, making shady offers. I walked very fast for what seemed miles, but passed only trees and bare lots where all the trees had been bulldozed down. I began to realize my folly when things sounding very much like coyotes began barking in the distance. Then I heard a muted roar, looked back, and saw a pair of car headlights approaching. *This is it,* I thought in absolute terror as the car slowed to a crawl beside me.

"Get in," he said.

Never have I been so overjoyed to see a black-and-white '57 Chevy with fat rear tires.

"No, thanks," I said coolly. "I'll walk."

"Look, I'm not gonna sit here and argue with you, just get the hell in the car."

I gave him some smart reply about how concerned he suddenly was over my welfare, whereupon he jerked on the brakes, got out, stomped around Tortoise, thrust me bodily into the car, slammed the door fiercely, and took off. I was about to make another even smarter remark when, without warning, we cruised into an absolute nest of police cars.

Three of them were stretched across Ross Road, with a big husky patrolman standing in the only remaining space big enough for a car to pass through.

"All right, son." He bent down, his hands on the window frame. "You want to pull over here?"

"Yes, sir," Truck said, and pulled over there.

"Let's see your license."

"Yes, sir," Truck said, pulling it out of his hip pocket.

The cop looked at it with a flashlight and said, "This is a Tennessee license. Where's your local license?"

"We just moved here, sir. I'm studying up on the booklet right now so I can take the test next week to get my Maryland license."

"Unh," the cop said. He walked around, taking a good look at Tortoise, and then returned to inquire why Truck had West Virginia license plates.

"My family moves around a lot, sir," Truck said.

The cop then shined his flashlight on me and asked to see my license. I believe those were the first words of actual business ever addressed to me by an officer of the law. I became completely undone, besieged by images of jail, fingerprints, slimy open toilets, police brutality.

"Show him your driver's license, Jeannie," Truck said gently. I took it out and handed it over, and he looked at it and looked at me and then back at it and finally gave it back and asked what we were doing out here.

"My girl and I were just taking a ride and we got kind of lost. Where does this road lead back in that direction?"

"It's going to lead to some big trouble in a few minutes," the cop said. "So you just take your girl and go out this way, and get you a local license, and get you some local plates, and stay away from those street races."

"Yes, sir," Truck said, and drove off slowly, looking back at the whole scene through the rearview mirror.

"Rule number one is, never talk back to a cop," he finally said in a sort of joking tone, which did not fool me for a minute. No amount of joking could hide the little bead of sweat that trickled down the side of his face and disappeared under the curve of his jaw. In my driveway, after chugging back all the way about twenty miles an hour, he finally just dropped the big front entirely. Closed his hand over mine and told me he was sorry, it was a stupid move to take me out there, but the way it happened I turned out to be a real live guardian angel.

"We got a pretty tough warning a couple weeks ago. If I'd been picked up in action back there I'd have lost my license for about fifty years."

"Well, I'm glad one thing worked out right."

"Look, I said I was sorry, didn't I? I was really going to play it straight tonight, so help me. It was just that Wally got my goat with that crack about staying at the Pit. I figured if we stayed there you'd have got the wrong idea. So we go out to Ross Road and you get the wrong idea. Wally and them are liable to get some pretty funny ideas, too, when I end up the only one that didn't get caught. Why don't we just forget the whole thing ever happened and go fishing tomorrow?"

Rule number two was, never be surprised by anything Truck Hardy might come up with in a tight situation.

"I can't go fishing, Truck. I don't know how to fish. I wouldn't know which end of the pole to hold. I'd scare all the fish away."

"The fish would scare you away, is what you mean."

It would be difficult to explain the combination of wheedling, harassing, and plain old green-eyed charm that eventually persuaded me to rise at the unheard-of hour of six o'clock on a Sunday morning to go fishing with Truck Hardy. In fact, I find it very difficult to explain the whole experience—all the crazy things he did to me that day up on the river, without even trying.

To begin with, he had to do everything *for* me, like threading a line through a rod and then attaching a sinker and bobber and hook out of the tackle box he had brought that seemed to contain at least one of everything that had ever been invented.

"Better keep an eye out for snakes too," he said casually, something I hadn't thought about until that moment. After that, however, the threat of snakes was never absent from my mind. I also found that I could do nothing but cringe and bury my face at the prospect of impaling a live minnow on a hook.

"You gotta be tough," he said. "You start feeling sorry for the bait, pretty soon you'll start feeling sorry for the fish you're trying to catch. Then what are you going to do when you get hungry?"

In other words, it was his scene all the way. For the first time, sitting on that log by that river, I knew the meaning of "babe in the woods." We were way up above the city, up above Great Falls even, farther north than I'd ever been on the Potomac before. Clean and quiet and not another soul anywhere around, only birds and insects and a little mist hovering about the tops of the trees.

As teachers go, he was a pretty patient one. He didn't just tell me things, he showed me. When we got to casting, for instance, he stood behind me with his hands grasping my hands, showing me how to flick my arm so that the hook plopped in the water between some rocks and overhanging trees. We had jumped from the bank to a rock and then onto another rock, so that by then we were standing right out in the river, with rocks and water and tree stumps on all sides.

"See? Just keep your eye on that cork. If you get a bite don't jerk too soon, give him a chance to get it in his mouth good and then give it a jerk to set the hook. Play him a little to tire him out before you haul him in. Got it?"

"Yes, yes, I got it," I assured him.

Actually, I didn't have it at all. I'm afraid my mind was on completely irrelevant things like the fact that his hands were on my hands, and he had on tennis shoes with no socks instead of cowboy boots, and his breath smelled like spearmint because we had eaten three packages of spearmint Lifesavers for breakfast driving up here.

On the very first cast, I got the line so hopelessly snarled around trees, rocks, and submerged stumps that after half an hour of fruitless labor Truck finally had to give up, cut the line loose, and start me over with a new hook, sinker, bobber and minnow.

I couldn't even manage to keep my feet on high ground. As soon as Truck turned his back, fishing by himself a few rocks over, I snagged my line again. I was trying to be cool, trying to untangle the line myself, when a dark snakelike creature glided past my elbow. I screamed, jumped backward, lost my balance, and fell into the water. It wasn't really dangerous, just humiliating. Especially since the snake turned out to be a submerged tree branch.

"Where's the rod and reel?" he demanded as he fished me out and deposited me back on the bank.

I pointed it out timidly. It had fallen off the rock and become entangled in the same clump of weeds as the hook, sinker, and bobber. The only way he could get it was to go in after it, which made him approximately as wet as me, not to mention slightly ripped off.

"Tell you what, Teach. I think you better just sit right there and don't move for the rest of the day."

"Where are you going?"

"I'm going upstream a little way where the fish haven't heard about you yet."

I watched him disappear around a bend and sat waiting for him, wet and tired and utterly miserable. Things kept crackling behind me and I envisioned all manner of beasts approaching, not only snakes but also bears, giant lizards, army ants.

What if he went off and left me?

What if he slipped and hit his head on a rock and drowned?

These and other terrible thoughts plagued me for what seemed like hours until I became thoroughly convinced that I would never see either him or the rest of the world again.

He finally came back to me, of course. Crunched through the underbrush like a big damp Adonis, bearing two nice-sized fish and looking considerably happier than when he left. Part of me flew to his side, a breathless heap of adoration clinging madly around his muscled waist. The rest of me sat unblinking on the log.

"You about ready for lunch?" he said.

"Lunch! I thought sure it must be time for dinner."

"Awwww. Cheer up, I brought you a present."

"What are those, catfish?"

"Bass," he said disdainfully. "Smallmouth bass."

"Wish I could have watched you catch them."

"If you'd been there I might not have caught them," he said, but only teasing.

"I'm sorry, really. I didn't mean to mess everything up. I just couldn't do anything right."

"Now you know exactly how I felt last night." He plopped down all his stuff and said, "You can watch me clean them, how's that?"

"You're really serious about eating those things?"

"We'll cook them first, if that'll make you feel any better. Why don't you scout around and bring back all the dry wood you can find. Oh yeah, and keep an eye out for snakes while you're at it." I threw a twig at him, which missed. He just laughed and went right on with what he was doing.

I'd never been much of a nature girl, but that afternoon something funny started going on between me and the ground and the sky as I sat back on my knees, watching him work. It absolutely knocked me out just watching the way his hands moved, so sure and easy. There was something incredibly real about it, something so simple and honest about catching a fish and building a fire, cooking it and eating it right there on the riverbank, just like that. I thought that if you could only strip away life's fat crust of sophistication—the big houses with wall-to-wall carpeting, the management consultants, and three-carbon college admissions applications—if you could only strip life to the bone, this is what you would come down to in the end, right here. All you really needed. Bent silently over the leaf-cluttered forest floor in tennis shoes with no socks, building a small ring of stones.

Boy, I was really gone.

Jeannie Travis, you are crazy, a little voice kept telling me—but oh, it felt so good. Gathering up branches to bring him like an offering, watching him form a careful teepee in the center. The fish were cleaned, their bellies slit, guts cast into the water. The tackle box had matches, folded-up sheets of tin foil to wrap the fish in.

"You city slicker," I said. "Using newfangled stuff like that." He threw a twig at me, which did not miss.

When the fish were done we sat side by side on the log and ate the sweet, flaky flesh right off the backbone, blowing it cool. It bore no resemblance to the soggy, tasteless seafood that came frozen from the supermarket.

"Show you a little secret," he said. "Here's the best part of the fish, right here." He peeled back a flap of skin and dug out a tiny hidden morsel, the cheek of the fish, and fed it to me with his fingers. There were four such morsels in all—three he fed to me and one he ate himself. No gourmet bachelor dinner with wine and candlelight and soft music could possibly have moved me to such a state of all-out, aching infatuation.

After he tossed the skeletons on the fire and poked the wood around to make it burn higher, he came back and stretched out on the ground next to me with his head resting against the log.

"Not going to fish any more?"

"What for, you still hungry?"

I shook my head slowly, no.

"Just wet, huh?" He grinned and tugged at my hair, damp and stringy.

"What's so funny?"

"You. Falling in the water like that. Reminds me of when I got baptized. Old Preacher Lowry, wading out in the river with a Bible in one hand and the back of my neck in the other, calling on the Lord to 'wash this sinner boy clean.' Grandpa and everybody standing on the bank dressed up fit to kill, singing hymns, me with my nose full of river water. I must've been about seven or eight and, hell, I was just calling on the Lord to keep old Preacher Lowry from drowning me. Wash this sinner boy clean, ha. I was good and clean for about two days, until I went and peeked underneath some little girl's dress at school and was right back being a sinner boy again. Just didn't stick, I reckon."

I told him about the way I was baptized, when I was twelve. I went to a Sunday School confirmation class and learned all the Christian doctrines, scriptures, catechisms, and creeds. When the session was completed, we were called up front during a special church service.

"I had a new hat, with flowers on it. The minister said some prayers and dipped his fingers in this silver dish of holy water and laid them on my head. Didn't even get my hair wet."

"Yeah, that figures."

"That's sort of the difference between you and me, isn't it."

"You mean, like, I'm a carpenter and you're a lady?"

Would you marry me anyway, would you have my baby?

Lord, I really must have been a little crazy. I reached for his hand, fishy and stubby and strong, held it up to my mouth, and kissed it. He didn't even seem surprised. He was always surprising me, but nothing I did ever seemed to surprise him. He didn't say a word—just laid his hand against my face, and drew me down to him, and kissed me. I'd received a fair share of kisses in my life, but that one was hard to believe.

"The difference between you and me, Miss Jeannie," he said finally, "is you're a girl and I'm a boy."

"I see what you mean," I said weakly, but he gave me one more anyway, just to make sure—tough yet soft at the same time, wet and warm and in no great hurry to end. Infatuation is a fragile spell, but he never broke it. It just kept lasting, all the way home.

"Well, Teach, what do you think?" he said, standing on my front porch with his hands in his pockets. It was only four-thirty, but it felt like four days. My father was out in the side yard, practicing his putt.

"I don't know," I said. I really didn't think anything. I could see and feel and smell and hear and taste all right, the thinking was just turned off. Like novocaine that works on the brain instead of the tooth. I wondered if it would hurt to start thinking again when it wore off, but it simply didn't wear off. Even when he said to meet him at the main clock between third and fourth periods the next day at school. Even after he left and I went up alone to my big plushy bedroom with the Peter Max bedspread and the Princess phone.

I rummaged through my records until I found the one I wanted, the golden oldies album, and listened to it lying on my bed looking around at all my thousands of things.

If I were a carpenter, and you were a lady,
Would you marry me anyway, would you have my baby?
If a tinker were my trade, would you still mind me?
Carrying the pots I made, following behind me?

Sing my love, through loneliness!
Sing my love, through sorrow!
I gave you my onlyness,
Give me your tomorrow.

Chapter 5

Senior Slump intoxicated different people in different ways. Some opted for alcohol, in appalling amounts and combinations, at certain local spots notorious for "letting you in on your library card." On Mondays there would always be great legendary tales about who had blown lunch all over whose car.

Others pursued different tangents. Kids who had formerly shown only stealthy interest in smoking grass now blossomed into daring public devotees of the weed, cool and hedonistic.

Sex remained the only truly private high around Albemarle, so that you still weren't really sure who was making it and who wasn't. I knew my friends were gradually beginning to wonder about me, even though my morals had always been considered second only to those of the Virgin Mary. What else could a girl like me possibly have in common with a guy like Truck Hardy? was everyone's attitude, which irked me a little. Good for them, I thought. Let them wonder.

"It's just, like Earl was saying last night, what are you trying to prove?" Trisha said one Saturday afternoon. We were lying out on our terrace covered with baby oil, getting some early May rays. Trisha was smoking a cigarette, coughing and making faces. For practice, she said. She had tried smoking pot a couple of times lately, but nothing much happened, and Eric had told her she was never going to be able to get really stoned until she learned to inhale deeply and hold it a long time, burned throat or no burned throat. So she had bought a pack of Camels, and she was practicing.

"The question is, Trisha, what are *you* trying to prove?"

"Nothing, I just figured it's something you should know how to do, that's all. Like drink a cocktail or play bridge. You have to be careful, is the only difference. Always know your source, so you don't end up with oregano, or bad stuff with speed or something in it. And of course cops and informers are everywhere, you have to watch out for them, too. Like, Eric Freeman himself could be a nark in disguise. You just have to know what you're doing."

She took a big drag and collapsed in a cloud of fumes and I thought the whole thing was pretty weird, taking up cigarette smoking so you could learn to smoke pot and get really stoned. I wasn't trying to make moral judgments—I simply couldn't imagine needing to go to all that trouble to get high. But then, as Oz had commented one day in English class, I acted like I was on a "natural high" these days all the time.

"I think you changed the subject," Trisha said.

"Repeat the question, please?"

"What is it with you and him? We can't figure it."

"It's something I think you should know how to do, that's all. Like drink a cocktail or play bridge."

"Come on, smart-mouth."

"I'm serious, Trisha. I think you should know how to accept someone who's different. I mean, we're very tolerant and liberal and we do a lot of talking about love and brotherhood and all that, but when you get right down to it we've been seeing pretty much what we want to see all our lives. You know what I'm saying? I mean, with Truck—it's so cool sometimes, being able to have fun with a guy who doesn't fit the old Ivy League law-school country-club mold. Just being able to relate as one human being to another, if nothing else. We could all stand to open our eyes that way a little."

I looked over at her but her eyes were protected by sunglasses at the moment, and very definitely closed.

"So what do your parents think of all this?"

I shrugged. "They like him fine, I guess. They don't tell me what to do, you know that."

Actually, it was a slight overstatement to say that my folks liked him fine. The big problem was that he worked a lot of nights until nine, and they thought nine-thirty was a very suspicious hour to be starting out on a date. Earl Corbett could have picked me up at midnight and brought me home at dawn, of course, but for Truck Hardy nine-thirty was borderline. I emphasized the fact that he was a decent, hard-working American boy. They emphasized the fact that, although they weren't trying to tell me what to do, they strongly suggested that I set my curfews at eleven o'clock on school nights, one o'clock on weekends. All right, I said finally, no great lover of hassles.

"Don't get me wrong, Jeannie," Trisha said. "I'm not trying to be nosy—the only thing is, we never see you any more! We just sometimes wonder, what do you two do? What kind of places does he take you?"

What was I supposed to tell her—the drive-in? Broom Creek Dragway? Riding around out in the country, just he and I and Tortoise and sometimes Davey, listening to country music?

I even listened to country music at home sometimes, tuning in Country Carl Barton on my clock radio when nobody else was around. "Make the World

Go Away" turned out to be some sort of country classic, which I decided was great in its own crazy way. And Johnny Cash and Merle Haggard, Hank Williams and Tammy Wynnette and Charlie Pride. Truck was right, they just said what they had to say, plain and simple. Songs of hard drinking and hard times and sometimes moving on, but mostly always love. Cheating love and happy love, departed love and love remembered. They hammered out a world, twangy and nasal and filled with the sliding whine of steel guitars, the unmistakable sound of heartbreak.

But somehow Country Carl's music never quite sounded the same at home on my AM-FM clock radio with the luminescent dials as it did on the road. To really feel it you had to be cruising along in a car like Tortoise, sitting as close as possible to a guy like Truck Hardy. Preferably at night, preferably along lonely stretches of rural highways, although neon-cluttered suburban strips would also do. It was novocaine for the brain all the time now: even college, that old sour weight on my mind, mellowed and didn't seem like such a big deal any more, one way or the other. September was only four months away, but it could have been four years for all I cared. Somebody else was in the driver's seat now, I was just a rider—and for the first time in my life I was going nowhere, doing nothing, for absolutely no logical reason.

"Jist hang awn tight, everythang gonna be aw *right*," as Country Carl was fond of saying.

"Well," I said slowly to Trisha, "for instance, we spend a lot of time working on his car. That is, he works on it. I mostly hand him things. Then on weekends whenever he can get off work we go out to this track where they have drag races."

"Drag races! Oh, come on, Jean."

"No, really. They're legal—they have an announcer's booth and bleachers and everything."

"Boy, that really sounds romantic."

Poor Trisha. I knew what she wanted to know, but there again, what could I say? I liked to think of Bubba Hardy kissing her just once, one good solid kiss, so she'd know what a real kiss felt like. I mean, Earl Corbett may have been the life of the party, but his kisses never exactly made the world go away.

"Then sometimes for real kicks," I said, trying to banter my way out of it, "we drive around and pick up hitchhikers."

My parents would have flipped if they had known that one. I nearly flipped myself the first time he did it. It was after school one day, during that first shaky week after the fishing trip, when I was still in the Jeannie-Travis-you-must-be-crazy stage. The boy hitchhiking was skinny and shabby and looked like he barely had enough strength to hold his thumb out.

"What are you doing?" I said when Truck pulled over and motioned to him.

"Scoot over. This guy might be Jesus in disguise."

"He also might be Mack the Knife! No telling what he's—"

"Thanks, buddy," the guy said, getting in and slamming the door. Truck swooped back into traffic. It turned out he wasn't Jesus or Mack the Knife either one; his name was Leon Kincheloe and he lived on a farm out in Prince George's County. Their pickup was broke down, he said. Till it got fixed he just had to hitch any time he wanted to get anyplace. "How far you-all going?"

"We'll take you all the way home, how's that?" Truck said. I clamped my teeth and stared out the window incredulously. "Long as you got a few chickens or something, so it looks like a farm. This little gal hasn't ever seen a chicken except in a bucket with slaw and rolls at one of those carry-out places."

Leon got a big toothy chuckle out of that one. "Yeah, we got chickens all right. Them plus a few goats and hogs and a cow. Old place ain't much though, I'll tell you that. Can't hardly make a living at it no more. The old lady, she works at the Pepsi place some to help out, but it's tough. They're not going to be able to hang onto it much longer."

"You don't have to tell me," Truck said. "I used to live on a farm some myself, outside Memphis. My grandfather's farm. I remember how it seemed like Memphis was hours away when I was a real little kid. Seemed like we had to drive all day to get there. Then Memphis got closer but the old farm just stayed the same. All these little towns all around started growing and houses went up and then they built a school right up against our south boundary, and a shirt factory on the other side, so pretty soon you couldn't look anywhere and see a tree any more. Drove that old man crazy. Hell, we weren't even making enough on the yield to cover the cost of harvesting it, but you know how an old farmer is. Said he wasn't going to sell, let the whole county sell out, he wasn't moving. Bank finally got us, of course."

"Yeah, them banks, they'll do it to you, all right."

"That really did finish him off, I mean, they had to put him in the state hospital. Right then, I swore I wasn't ever going to get attached to anything the way that old man got attached to that farm. If they can come and take it away from me, man, I don't want it. Nobody can get you if you're traveling light."

We were heading into farmland, remote and lonely. Pretty lousy place to be stuck with a broken-down pickup, I thought. I must admit I was sulking, feeling a little piqued that Truck would tell all these things to a stranger that he'd never even mentioned to me. I didn't feel much better when we finally pulled into a long gravel driveway beside a small frame house that looked as if it hadn't been painted in two centuries. The barn, in maybe three centuries.

Truck opened the door and got out like these were

his best friends or something. Chickens fluttered around and scurried under the porch going *bawwwwk, bawwwwwk*. He and Leon were halfway to the barn before they remembered me.

"Kind of watch where you step," Leon said.

Hanging over the livestock pens, Truck breathed deeply and ran his hands over the worn, patched fence. Hadn't smelled that smell in a long time, he said. To me it didn't seem like anything to get excited about. The goats smelled terrible and the hogs smelled worse, and it was a treat to finally get inside the barn where at least it smelled like straw.

"Is that the pickup?" Truck said, pointing to a rusty gray truck parked to one side.

"Yeah, that's her. Just won't start. Been sluggish for a good bit now, but the other morning she plumb wouldn't start."

"Mind if I take a look?"

"Go right ahead. I never was too good at fixing things. I been meaning to have this old boy up the road come down and see what he can do, but just haven't got around to it."

Meanwhile Truck wasn't wasting any time. "You got a screwdriver or something? It's nothing much, you just weren't getting any spark, that's all. Points on your distributor are about shot." I could tell by the look on Leon's face that he didn't know much more about the points on his distributor than I did. Truck fiddled around and it couldn't have been more than five minutes before he had it running. "Least this'll get you to a garage to get a new set of points."

"Fella, you are somethin'," Leon said, shaking his head in dazed admiration. "How'd you like to feed the stock and milk Gloria?" Gloria, he added for my benefit, was the cow.

"Tell you what," Truck said. He was in his element, no doubt about it. "You feed the stock and I'll milk Gloria."

Leon told him sure, any time, just come around every day and fix up what's broken and do all the chores if that was his idea of a hobby. He got the milking stool and moved Gloria around in her stall. At first she didn't look too happy about the strange pair of hands pulling and tugging at her udder, but Truck soon snowed Gloria too. The milk came out in sharp, foamy *brrrip, brrrrrips* into the pail. Sure had been a long time, he said.

"Is there anything you can't do?" I said as we trundled out of their driveway at last with Leon waving a grateful farewell.

"Yeah, two things," he said. He reached and pulled me over so I was sitting close enough to put his arm around. Driving with one hand, and he's doing about sixty-five on a one-lane country road. "The first thing is, I can't pass English. And the second thing is, I can't figure out what you're mad about."

"I'm not mad, Truck, it's just—"

"What?"

"I don't know, you just keep springing these things on me. You know so many things, why do you act the way you do around school?"

"How do I act?"

"Oh, I don't know. Tough, hostile. Dumb. You know how you act. Saying 'ain't' all the time."

"Come on, Teach. What do you want me to do, run around hollering, 'Look at me, I know how to milk a cow?' Half those kids at Albemarle don't even know what a cow is. They think milk grows in wax cartons at the grocery store."

"That's not what I mean."

"I act the way I do so people will leave me alone. You go around telling everything you know, pretty soon people expect you to know everything."

"You sell yourself short, is your trouble."

"My trouble is, I don't sell myself at all. Turning cartwheels for the fans, up for auction on the block, send a kid to camp. You ought to be a missionary, is what you ought to be. You remind me of what's-his-name, that crazy guy telling how he's going to stand out in the field catching little kids who fall off the cliff."

"Catcher in the Rye? Are you talking about *Catcher in the Rye?*"

"Yeah, something like that."

"I thought you'd never read but one book."

He grinned. "Oh, well. I only read *Catcher in the Rye* because of all the dirty words in it."

"I'll tell you what I think about you, boy." It really killed me, the way he kept springing things on me. "I think you could do anything in this world you wanted to do. I think you could pass college-prep English if you half tried, and in fact I think you could be a damn Ph.D. in English, if you worked at it."

"The way you say it is, 'If you would just apply yourself, Lamar, you could really go places.' You got to learn to talk like that if you're going to be a teach."

"You *could* go places."

"What kind of places?"

"I'd like to hit you, you know that?"

"Go ahead."

I hit him on the shoulder with my fist, put my whole five-foot-four, hundred and five pounds into it, not to mention the chunky "peace" ring on the third finger of my hand.

"Ouch," he said.

I hit him again.

"If I get me one of them there Ph.D.'s in English and promise not to say 'ain't' no more, will you marry me?"

"*Yes.*"

He screeched out a long rebel yell, eeeEEE-HAH, and drove on.

Chapter 6

And of course the drag racing. How could you explain to somebody about the drags?

Well, you see Trisha, it's like this—these two cars line up at the start line on either side of the "Christmas tree." It has nothing to do with Christmas, Trisha, it's what they call this pole with lights on it that signals the drivers when to start. There are about four yellow lights that blink down from the top, like On Your Mark, Ready, Set, and finally the green light at the bottom flashes, that means Go, so both cars blast off down this quarter-mile track and the first one over the finish line wins!

No, no, I thought. No point even trying to explain it in mere words, she would just have to go and see it for herself. And even then she couldn't possibly see it like I saw it, she wouldn't have Bubba Hardy leading her around by the shoulders.

He took me out to Broom Creek the very next Saturday after our fishing trip. It was out in the country, just far enough from the city to give you the feeling of really going somewhere, a little track surrounded by cornfields, with rolling farmland all around.

On the surface there wasn't a whole lot to it, just a wide asphalt "pit" area for working on cars, and a two-lane fenced-off strip for racing cars, and bleachers on both sides for the fans.

The cars themselves were the real spectacles. That day they were running everything from Volkswagens and pickup trucks to wild-looking Fords and Plymouths with elaborate iridescent paint jobs and names scrolled across their sides like "Bushwacker" and "Super Duster" and "Mule Man."

"Nothing special today," Truck said. "No trophies or anything, just time trials and record runs and stuff."

"Well, then, basically, what's the purpose of it?"

"Beg pardon?"

"I mean, you know, what's the point?"

"Oh, I don't know, Teach. What's the point of anything? Just the fun of winning, I reckon. The satisfaction of breaking a track record, or maybe even a national record sometimes. Just doing the best you can with what you got is what it boils down to. You got to run in your class, see. A given engine can only go so fast, so the idea is to run as good as you can within your set of limitations. Sometimes it comes right down to how good your reflexes are, against the other guy's. Now Tortoise, he's in a Modified Production class—that means he's faster than some but not as fast as others. For instance, he can't go as fast as those 'funny cars' out there that are nothing but engines with painted-up fiberglass frames. That's not my idea of a car. Or those rail jobs, either, nothing but an engine and wheels and a roll bar. They don't even burn regular gas. Shoot, you get an F4 Phantom jet out there it would win a trophy, too, but that's not the point. Guess it all depends on what you like, but me, my idea of a car is a streetable, something you can drive to Sunday School as well as cream everybody on the quarter-mile. Something you can use for everthing."

"Everything?" I teased.

"Yeah, everything." He rumpled my hair, then ran his hand over Tortoise's shiny black flank and said, "Fifty-seven Chevy's a real classic. Kind of like old Humphrey Bogart movies, might not look so sleek compared to the newer stuff, but people always love to see 'em anyway."

This was no exaggeration. As soon as we got over to the pits and Truck raised the hood, a steady stream of friends and rivals started dropping by to pay their respects, including the lady who sold patches and decals and hot dogs at the Snakshak and "Mean Mike," a friendly state highway patrolman. The one I liked best, though, was Pop Summers, a burly middle-aged man who greeted Truck with a slap on the back that would have knocked anybody else flat on the ground.

"Pretty!" he kept saying, with his head stuck under the hood. "Mighty pretty. If you lived up around these parts, Hardy, you'd be putting me out of a job."

Pop was one of the founding fathers of Broom Creek, Truck told me after he left. He did a little officiating, a little announcing, and owned a pretty large hunk of the place. Also ran a nice garage business a little farther up county, he added, and pointed out to me the '62 Chevy with "Pop's Speed Shop" on one fender that Pop set up personally and sponsored in races all over the East.

Meanwhile, there were all these guys in jeans and T-shirts hanging over Tortoise's sides admiring the engine and exclaiming over the fact that Truck had built it all himself, part by part, so that he knew how each thing fit together and worked like the fingers and knuckles and joints on his own hand.

The conversation centered around the "wild juice set-up to feed those dual quads" and the "hairy lift on that cam" and his "outasight set of tuned headers." As for me, I kept my mouth shut and my ears open and came out of it with a new respect for Truck's intellect: you'd have to be a genius, I figured, just to understand what all those guys were talking about. He tried to explain things to me, but it was too much for one girl for one day, and in the end I was perfectly content to be his little robot assistant—handing him things as he disconnected the tailpipe from the muffler and put on the slick rear tires—just basking in the noisy, greasy mystery of it all.

"Guarantee you one thing," he remarked at one point, exchanging the "dwell meter" he was through with for the "timing light" I was holding, "I got the best-looking crew of anybody out here."

This made for a very nice moment, considering it was the mushiest thing he had ever said to me.

He also paid a good many compliments to Tortoise —talking earnestly to his engine block, patting his radiator cap, reminding him of things to keep in mind. So that by the time we were finished and he moved down into the staging lanes with the big E/MP classification painted on his windshield, Tortoise seemed practically human to me, and Truck Hardy somewhat more than human, and I didn't need to ask what was the point of it any more. The point was, very simply, that I was totally *with* that boy and that car, and I was dying to see them sweep everybody right off the track. I would never have believed I could get so fired up watching Lamar P. Hardy drive a '57 Chevy down a quarter-mile strip—yet there I was, hanging over the fence by the finish line like it was my survival at stake instead of a Broom Creek class record and some stubborn male pride.

There were a lot of minor casualties on the strip that day, guys blowing engines and dropping transmissions and disqualifying themselves with false starts— but never Truck. He made nine runs in all, smooth and clean, and he never jumped the light, never fishtailed on takeoff, and never blew a shift. After each one he would drive back around to the pits and get his E.T.—meaning, Elapsed Time—and then come tell me and I would write it down. He was turning in nice little times, he said—11.65, and 11.52, and even one 11.49. Calculated in seconds and hundredths of seconds, you understand.

"To give you a better idea," he said once, "it works out around 119 miles an hour."

"A hundred and nineteen miles an hour!"

"Well, maybe 118."

He even ran against a few cars in higher classes—which is to say, faster—and beat them all the way up to the "C-gasser" category when a 427 Corvette named "Glass Rat" finally nosed him out at the finish line. There was a lot of clapping after that run, and I had a feeling it was for Truck instead of the guy who won.

It was nearly dark by then, and the pits were scattered with guys connecting their tailpipes back up and putting on their street tires, getting ready to head home. While he did the big stuff, Truck said, he would let me wipe the numbers off the windshield and the dust off Tortoise's hood and top and fenders.

"And just for being such a good crew," he said finally, as we wound slowly down the driveway and onto Route 34, "I'm going to take you to this little old honky-tonk up the road and buy you the biggest plate of barbecue they got. Bet you never been to a honky-tonk before."

No, I admitted, couldn't say I had ever been to a honky-tonk. "But then, before today I'd never been to a drag race, either."

"That's what I like about you, Teach—you remind me of a baby chick just stepping out of its shell with its feathers still wet, all legs and eyes and mouth, never been much of anywhere so the barnyard looks great."

I was about to take issue with this comparison when we crunched into the gravel parking lot of a nondescript, weathered roadhouse with an orange neon sign that said "Buck and Bee's—Good Eats—ABC On and Off."

Buck and Bee's, contrary to appearances, turned out to be the Brown Derby of local drag racing. Not only were the eats extremely good, but also everybody who was anybody around Broom Creek came in sooner or later that night, and most of them stopped by our booth to at least say hi. When Pop Summers came in, he even sat down with us for a while and bought us a beer. I never had been a great beer fan, but I drank it because Pop bought it—he was that kind of a guy.

"Where you been hiding all winter, Hardy? I was planning to put you on the payroll. Had to paint every one of those bleachers myself."

"Trying to pass history and English so I can graduate," Truck told him. "I finally found me a little gal knows how to read and write—figure maybe some of it'll rub off on me."

Pop leaned over to me and said, "All you got to know to win this fella's heart, honey, is how to outclass a 327-cubic-inch Chevy engine."

They chatted a little longer—about gear ratios, and clutch and flywheel setups, and whether Pop was going to run in the June Point Series meet up at York. There was something special between them, anybody could have seen it, and when Pop finally drank up and said "take care" and moved on to somebody else's table it was beautiful the way Truck looked at him, following him with his eyes.

"There's a good man," he said. "Give you the shirt off his back. Been married twenty years but never had any kids of his own."

All this time the jukebox had been coming out with one fantastic old song after another. I mean Buck and Bee had very classical taste in music—really golden oldies like dreamy slow Elvis and Platters and Everly Brothers songs from the late 1950s.

I bless the da-a-a-ay I found you, crooned Don and Phil from their younger short-haired days,

> *I want to stay around you,*
> *Now and forever—*
> *Let it be me!*

"Fifty-seven." Truck grinned. "Sure was a good year for Chevys and music." He finished his beer and then he finished my beer and asked me if I wanted to dance, which I did; even though nobody else was dancing I discovered that I really wanted to dance. There wasn't even a dance floor, but at Buck and Bee's it didn't matter, it was just a little honky-tonk sitting by the highway in the middle of cornfields, and if you wanted to get up and dance right there between the jukebox and the bar there wasn't a single person in the place who cared.

"What you want to go to college for anyway?" he murmured comfortably against my hair.

"Did I say I wanted to go to college?"

"Spend four more years sitting in classes reading a bunch of books about what the world's all about, when you could be finding out for yourself firsthand."

"I'm just waiting for somebody to come up with a better idea."

"O.K., here's one. You can come along with me and be my partner. If I had me an English teacher on my crew I could promote myself a little, write some letters to some companies, all the words spelled right and everything. That's what you got to do if you want to make a living at it—like, 'Dear Firestone, I'm Truck Hardy, my car's Tortoise, here's some records I set, some pictures of us in action. You keep me in tires and I'll wear your decal, advertise your product at tracks all up and down the Eastern seaboard.' Then when you really get good they give you a little dough, too, in case you might be thinking of switching over to Goodyear.

There's all kinds of angles, once you get into it. You meet people, establish contacts, get written up in racing magazines and newspapers. Maybe get offers or invitations to travel around to different shows and exhibitions. I can always do a little free-lance engine work on the side, too, if things get tight. Just take it as it comes, one day at a time, we could make it."

"Sounds great. Where are we supposed to live all this time?"

"Oh, I don't know. Different places. Probably a trailer or camper van while we're on the road. We could be like a turtle—a real tortoise—carry our house right with us. There's campgrounds everywhere you go in this country, with bathhouses even. You could take a bubble bath every night if you wanted."

"Bubble bath nothing—I think we should take baths only in creeks and rivers, and never eat anything except fish we catch ourselves, plus maybe a few berries, and camp right out in the open air in sleeping bags."

"How about, in *a* sleeping bag?" he suggested with a charming little smile. All I can say is, don't ever try to out-bull Bubba Hardy.

"Come on," he said, "let's go."

"Let's go where?"

"I don't know, let's just go. Poor old Tortoise is getting lonesome parked out there all by himself."

So we paid up and crunched back outside with our arms around each other's waists, and the sky was full of stars.

"Hey, there's Pop's trailer," he said. "Come on, you don't believe me. I'll show you how easy it is to be a turtle."

"Just open the door and walk in?" I said hesitantly.

"Sure, he's in there drinking beer with Buck, he won't care."

It was so compact and efficient, that was the beauty of it—crisp checked curtains at the windows, lavatory and toilet and shower all combined, a lounge that was seats by day and beds by night, with a table that folded right up into the wall.

"See this? A sink with its own water tank, and a butane stove, and an icebox cooled by good old-fashioned ice. Come here a minute," he insisted, rummaging through a cabinet. "Hold this frying pan right here, let's see how you look."

"You're nuts, you know that?"

"Yeah, man, that's great. Where's a mirror? That's beautiful."

"You're really out of your tree," I kept telling him —but the damage was already done, doors opening in my head, life looking like a multiple-choice question all of a sudden, all sorts of trouble. Like, who said you had to have a countertop range and eye-level oven, electric can opener and pop-up toaster and waffle iron, eight-speed blender and stand-up freezer and disposal and jet-action percolator just to cook breakfast for a man?

He put his arms around me from behind and started laying little kisses on the back of my neck and I said, with a valiant attempt at calmness, "I guess this is what you meant that day when you were talking about traveling light."

"Mmm-hmm," he said. He really had this incredible way of blowing your hair aside and kissing the back of your neck so that shivers ran all up and down not only your spine but also your arms and legs, not to mention the hair along your arms raising up with goose bumps and your stomach plus a few other places sort of melting and running all together. "This is exactly what I meant when I was talking about traveling light."

Chapter 7

On the way out to Broom Creek there was an antique place, a large white house with a barn in back and a neat sign out front saying: "Antiques, J. R. Monk, We Buy and Sell." Every time we passed I wanted to stop, and finally I bugged Truck about it so much he gave in one Sunday morning and pulled in the long cobbled driveway.

"What's your story, now, you buying or selling?"

"Just browsing," I said. Dreaming, was actually more like it. I had acquired my own little vision of what life could be like. I mean, a mechanic was O.K., nothing at all wrong with a race driver or a mechanic, but an artisan was something else! You might say I was a person of endless stubborn visions.

When the guy came out on the porch and asked could he help us, Truck told him, with a perfectly straight face, that we were newlyweds and we had a little garage apartment, nothing fancy, but a place we wanted to fill with some odd pieces that would be practical as well as ornamental. After this dazzling line of bull he turned to me with a shy, loving, new-groom look and I nearly broke up on the spot. About this time a car full of old ladies drove in so Mr. Monk walked us to the barn and told us to make ourselves at home, just take our time, he would be right with us.

Truck looked around at the stacks of dusty things thrown all helter-skelter and said, "You don't wanna be in the antique business, Teach, believe me."

"Yes, I do."

"You think it's all fun and games, you don't know how much work it is. How'd you like to go around dusting a dozen spindleback benches and five hundred porcelain slop jars every day?"

"I'd love it."

"For about a week you'd love it. Listen, not only do you have to travel all over back roads conning people out of their old stuff, you also got to haul it around everywhere, clean it up, fix it if it's broken—man, it's hard work refinishing furniture. Shellac and sand, shellac and sand, you feel like your arm's gonna fall off. Then you got to sell it—you tell some guy it costs a hundred and he says he'll give you sixty, then you say I might go ninety-five and he says not a penny over seventy and by the time you finally get his eighty-two bucks you've earned every cent of it. Plus you got capital invested, overhead, maintenance, fire insurance, termites, everything hanging like a big yoke around your neck—just the opposite of traveling light."

I remained blissfully unmoved by all these facts. I kept hearing imaginary conversations in my head, my mother talking to my aunt in New Jersey: *Yes, well, they're doing fine. They have a little place out in the country, a couple of horses, he's in the antique business. He's a different kind of person, not the sort of boy we pictured Jeannette ending up with, but she's very happy —she takes courses on the side toward her degree, you know. She has three semesters left. And you should see the gorgeous things they have in their home. He's a real artist, you'd be amazed at what he can do with old pieces you'd throw out for junk.*

Long summer days spent touring the countryside looking for salvageable pieces, always on the prowl for new sources. Then long winter nights in front of a stone fireplace, polishing and waxing rare old spinning wheels and blanket chests in an atmosphere warm with copper and wormy oak, hooked rugs on the floor, and upstairs a big fourposter with a patchwork quilt I'd made myself.

"Tell me what all these things are," I insisted as we trooped through the jumbled array of wooden and china treasures, butter churns and spice boxes, chairs and more chairs and fancy carved cupboards, lamps with leaded glass and milk-glass shades.

"A pain in the neck, that's what all these things are."

"Look at the cute little cradle," I said. He said he'd rather not. "What do you think the value of that is?"

"I don't know about that, but come over here and I'll show you the value of this cute little sofa." He pulled me down across his lap and I escaped only to get caught again in a maze of caneback chairs stacked precariously in one corner. A few minutes later, when Mr. Monk came into the barn with the old ladies, Truck dragged me behind a tall oak wardrobe and tickled me in the ribs without mercy the whole time they were there, trying to make me laugh out loud.

"Will you just look at the legs on that lovely piece?" this one old lady kept saying, and Truck would poke his head down, look at my legs, and give me a wicked nod before returning to my ribs.

We sneaked out even before the old ladies had left, actually, since we were on our way out to Broom Creek and Truck was always in a big hurry on his way out to Broom Creek.

"No, man, antiques—that's not hairy and noisy and fast enough. That's something you do when you're old and gray."

"You'll be old and gray some day. You don't think so now, but you will."

"O.K., tell you what. We'll race and do cars till I'm old and gray, about fifty or so, then we'll take what we got and put it into antiques."

"How about thirty years old?"

"No way, not a day under forty."

"Thirty-five?"

"Thirty-nine and a half. That's it."

"You drive a hard bargain."

"Yes or no, is it a deal?"

He was such a tease, so much fun to give in to. "O.K.," I said, "it's a deal," and we kissed on it.

It was surprising how this idea of staying with him took hold of me, this feeling of always being with him. And if not as Mrs. Lamar Puckett Hardy, then why not simply as Jeannie Travis? "Teach," his mate, his partner, his girl, his woman.

All those ambitious plans for my future, the ones I had taken for granted for so long, beginning with the Holyoke education! Then maybe a graduate degree. Certainly a few years as a swinging single girl with a dynamic teaching job before some doctor or architect would cruise along in a Porsche to wine me and dine me and marry me in a splendid burst of flowers. They faded so quickly, all those adolescent visions, from technicolor to black and white and finally to nothing at all, as Truck moved in and completely took over my head with his own gritty brand of reality.

Of course I took great pains to speak casually of him around the house, but it was not so easy to be casual about it at school, especially considering he was the chief reason I went to school any more. My brainy college prep classes gradually became just the long, boring periods in between the five-minute breaks. During these breaks I would wait for him or he would wait for me and we would stand there, wherever our paths happened to cross, right in the middle of the hall like rocks in the middle of a river. Anybody who wanted to get by just had to steer around us. He would maybe give me a piece of gum or something and I would show him pictures I had drawn in my notebook of Tortoise. Once I worked for a week on a '57 Chevy drawn by a mammoth team of horsepower, 365 horses. I drew each horse in tiny detail and counted them to make sure I had 365.

Naturally with all this important business to transact I would occasionally fail to hear the bell ring. I wouldn't realize it until the halls started thinning out with just a couple of kids dashing for their classrooms and then I'd be a little late for my own classes. My friends would look at me and look at the teacher and look at each other and one day Mrs. Burkowitz, my Music Appreciation teacher, was in a bad mood and sent me down to the office for a late slip. Mrs. Farragut gave me the funniest look, like *Jeannette Travis? Late slip?* When I got back to the classroom I couldn't keep a straight face, I just took a seat in the back and tried to listen to the music Mrs. Burkowitz was playing that day, something weird like "The Rite of Spring." Personally I didn't like it much but to each his own, I figured.

The mornings weren't so bad, but in the afternoons I would sit in class and look at the clock and listen for the ticks—it made a big *tick* every time a minute went by. And Fridays were impossible. On Fridays I would think, *two o'clock now, another hour and a half till school's out and he drives me home, that gives me about three hours to wash my hair and dry it before dinner, then three more hours to get dressed and maybe read a little English before he picks me up at nine-thirty, then all that messing around with Wally and those guys, add another hour and a half for that, that makes nine hours in all before the beer is gone and the jokes all told and the first movie over and everybody leaves and we're alone, only nine more hours.*

When things were like that in the middle of the day with hundreds of people milling around clanging lockers, you can imagine what it was like when we were alone. It was almost scary, the way he turned on feelings in me that I'd never even known I had—feelings that had certainly never been hinted at by my mother or *Lost Along the Way*.

The first time he slipped his hand underneath my clothes and really touched me, he excited me so much that it embarrassed me and I asked him to stop, please stop, and he did. Even if he didn't like it much, he understood.

"What are you ashamed of?" he said patiently. "Or is it you *still* think I bite?"

He got out of the car and went to the Snack Bar then, returning after an interminable time with some popcorn and my favorite kind of ice-cream bar. "Here you go, Teach, this'll cool you off."

I watched him unwrap it for me, his face soft and teasing in the flickering lights of the movie, and I had to laugh at myself a little. And at those desultory stars of *The Devil Takes a Mate* galloping across the screen. And at my friends, for wondering how on earth I could possibly fall for the biggest hood in the whole school.

It wasn't ten minutes until we were leaning together again, kissing each other with popcorn-and-ice-cream breath, really hopeless. And I let him go a lot longer that time before I finally had to stop him.

"Why?" he kept whispering. "What are you so afraid of?" Although he knew good and well why, and what I was afraid of. I knew how much he wanted it but I couldn't help it, that one last step was just too much, and too soon.

"O.K.," he said, not very calmly. "All right, O.K. Let's talk about—Shakespeare. You want to talk about Shakespeare? Come on. Tell me everything you know about Shakespeare."

He never really pressured me, but it began to cause

friction, more and more as time went on, because the things that excited and satisfied me only frustrated him. A couple of times when it was really bad he wanted me to touch him to help him get relief, and I tried but I was awkward about it. It seemed unnatural and strange to me, and it was never right. And the one time it was almost right for him something happened at the last minute, someone walked past the car and banged on the roof and said, *"Give it to her, man!"* or something like that and it ruined everything. It was terrible. He just sat up and took a couple of really deep breaths and started the car and took me home right then.

"Look," he said, "I'd rather not even hold hands or anything than go through that any more, no kidding." Which we tried the next time we went out, and found to be much easier said than done.

It all came to a head one bad, rainy night near the end of May when he called and broke a date. He'd been acting funny for a couple of days, and when he called with this fishy-sounding story about having to stay home with Davey I just came right out and told him, look, I sort of figured he might want to date another girl, so if it was another girl tonight, why didn't he just say so?

"It's not another girl, damn it. I wish it was some other girl. I told you, I have to stay here with Davey because the old lady's working and Mary Lynn's got a date with this guy she's crazy about. He's supposedly going to marry her as soon as he gets his divorce, so I told her I'd babysit a couple times if it would help get her married off. What do you want to do, come over here and see for yourself? Sit around this crummy place and help me babysit or something?"

"Yes."

I knew better than that, but I wanted to be with him. It was raining like mad and my parents had gone to a dinner party and I just didn't feel like being alone.

Waiting for him to pick me up, I brushed my hair down loose around my face the way he liked it, and I put on this clingy little jersey dress I had that I'd never been able to wear much of anywhere because the skirt was too short and the neckline too low. I knew better than that, too, but that's the kind of mood I was in. Really on the brink. Wondering if there wasn't a way I could be some other girl, just for one night.

What I failed to realize was the kind of mood *he* was in. It wasn't so bad while Davey was still awake, because we were playing with him and building things on the floor with these colored blocks of his and cooking little frozen pizzas in the oven. But then Truck put Davey to bed and I picked up the blocks and went into the kitchen to check on the pizzas. I was trying to clean up their incredibly messy kitchen a little and in a minute he came and stood leaning in the doorway watching me.

"I like your dress," he said. "What there is of it." He was barefooted and had on these crummy-looking, faded jeans and after a minute he lit up a Lucky Strike and said, "You don't have to bother with that mess. Quit working so hard, why don't you? Come on in here and sit down."

But the pizzas were just about ready, I told him, trying my best to sound unruffled, and did he want me to cut them in halves or leave them whole or what?

"I don't think I want any pizza right now," he said, which irked me a little since I had just finished cooking all these pizzas which I certainly didn't feel like eating either.

"What's the matter, don't you feel well or something?"

"I feel all right. How do you feel?"

"I thought you were the one who wanted pizza, Truck. What do you want if you don't want pizza?"

"If you would ever get the hell out of the kitchen

I would show you what I want." He walked over and took the spatula out of my hand and started crisscrossing me with little slicing motions. "I want you," he said softly, dividing me into neat little six-inch sections. "Without mushrooms or sausage or anything, just you."

He knew exactly how to go about it, too. He started kissing me with his mouth wide open, holding my whole head between his hands, and before we ever got out of the kitchen he had me shaking all over and saying, "Don't, Bubba, please," which sounded so feeble and absurd set against that background of two bedrooms and three empty beds and double locks on the door and no one expected home for hours.

"Oh, baby, why not?" he kept breathing in my ear, driving me right up the wall. "I swear I'll be careful, if that's what you're worried about."

It would have been so much simpler if pregnancy was the only thing to be afraid of. But there was much more, a whole tangle of other things like guilt and self-respect and reputation, and that old nagging fear of being taken for a big ride and then put down in the end. Stupid hangups, maybe—built up by all those years of lectures and movies and warnings—but very real. And not so easy to shrug off. And even harder to put into words.

I tried to tell him, I really did try to explain why I just wasn't ready to get into things that deeply with anyone. But it came out sounding so ridiculous, and I felt so ridiculous, and it was just a bad, bad scene.

"Not *ready*. God, Jeannie, how long you figure it's going to take?"

"I don't know, Bubba, I guess—not until it means as much to you as it means to me."

"Oh, man." I could've been a porcupine, the way he suddenly dropped me and turned away. "I need you about like I need another pain in the ass, you know that?" He reached for the phone, dialed a number, and asked for a cab sent to Lake Pleasant Towers.

"Please, wait a minute—"

"Wait a minute, nothing. You get your shoes on and get yourself and that goddamn dress downstairs in the lobby to wait for the cab, because if you stay up here sixty seconds longer you're liable to get laid whether you like it or not. Screwy little brainy bitch. Yes, I don't want it, no, I do want it, don't know what you want. I've seen a lot of brainy bitches, but you're the screwiest."

"Thanks. Thanks a lot for everything."

"And do yourself another big favor," he called after me down the hall. "From now on, if you don't want to fight the bull just stay the hell out of the ring."

Thankfully, my parents weren't home yet. I paid the taxi driver and went straight upstairs to bed. Threw all my clothes on the floor, including that damn dress, and didn't even turn on the light. Stanley readjusted himself around my feet and I lay there rigid with rage and frustration at the awful dead-endedness of it. It had happened before and it was going to happen again, every time now, put out or get lost, sugar, yes or no— there wasn't anywhere else left for us to go. Such a lousy end to come to.

I thought I would never get to sleep but I guess I did, because my phone woke me up some time in the middle of the night, maybe two or three o'clock, ringing on the little toadstool table right beside my bed. I reached it before it rang again. There was a muddled nasal voice and several tinny clangs as forty-five cents was deposited from not too long a distance.

"Hi," he said. He was calling from this phone booth, and did I know where Route 29 crossed Route 34? Well, that's where he was, only a little bit north of there. He was at a gas station and he had this broad waiting in the car, so he couldn't talk too long. The gas station was closed, and everything else was closed, and Tortoise did not like this broad at all. He was idling funny and kept choking out. In fact, I was the only goddamn girl Tortoise had ever liked. He never did anything ornery when I was in the car.

I was a little groggy and it took me a few minutes of this stuff to realize he was pretty well sloshed.

"Hey look," he went on. "I'm sorry what I said tonight."

"That's all right, Truck, but I really can't talk now."

"Hey, I know you're mad because I called you a screwy bitch. I didn't mean that. You know why I said it, but it's all right now."

"I'm not mad, Truck, I'm just afraid my parents will wake up."

"O.K. but wait, don't go yet. I have to tell you something I thought of tonight."

I closed my eyes and listened to the sound of his voice and thought how strange it was. I had always wondered about people I saw making phone calls late at night from isolated booths. Wondered what kind of people they were, and who they were calling, and what it was they had to say that couldn't wait until morning.

"Like, do you remember tonight, when you were building that junk with Davey's blocks and he kept telling you this is the house and this is the car and the car goes to the store and all that stuff. Well, I decided you should be a kindergarten teacher or something, and teach little kids, because I think you'd be better. Teaching little kids. Like remember how you never got mad at him or nothing, you acted like you were interested and kept asking him questions back. That's what I mean, you gotta be a good teacher, Jeannie, not a 'this is not a complete sentence' and all that crap kind of a teacher. You gotta be good."

"All right, Bubba. I will, honest, I will." He could

really get you, Bubby Hardy could. Drunk or sober, without even trying.

"Because I had this really nice teacher once, I never told you about her. I told you I never had nothing but bad teachers but I forgot about Mrs. Leslie and I just thought of her tonight, because you reminded me of her. It was the fifth grade and her name was Mrs. Leslie. And she was kind of fat, but she always smelled nice, and we had this science report to write—"

"Your three minutes are up, sir," I heard the operator say, then some muffled swearing and more coins clanging.

"So I didn't know what to do, you know, because I was new in that school, Christ, we was always moving around. So I had this box of flies I had tied, I used to do that. Tie flies, you know what that is?"

"I don't think so."

"They look like little bugs, but fancier, you use them for fishing lures. Different from the kind of fishing we did up on the river. I'll take you fly fishing some day, I swear I will, Jeannie. But Mrs. Leslie. She really liked those goddamn flies. She asked me all this stuff about what different ones did and then pretty soon she let everybody in the class come up to see them and I explained about how you did it so the fish would think they were bugs. Mrs. Leslie said that was a scientific hobby and I was big man in class that day, let me tell you. She never flunked me or nothing, and I never wrote any science report. Then she said maybe other people had scientific hobbies so pretty soon all the kids started bringing in their mice and worm hatchers and one kid had an ant farm and one poor little crippled girl, she wore goddamn leg braces, and only in the fifth grade, she brought these carrots she was growing in a pot."

I put the covers over my head and closed my eyes and had him with me, right there with me.

"And then one day the principal came in and said

the place looked like a zoo and anyway they had these rules, so Mrs. Leslie said we had to take the stuff all home. Hey, Jeannie?"

"I'm still here."

"The thing is, I have to go now. I just wanted to tell you that stuff before I forgot it. I hope you're not mad. It's going to be all right, I'm telling you. This girl in the car, man. You won't believe this. You really got me messed up good. I had to close my eyes and think about you, was the only way. I mean, Christ, I never loved anybody before but I think I must love you. Don't laugh, Jeannie, but goddamn, I love you."

I wasn't laughing. Believe me, I wasn't laughing. I wasn't doing anything. Just lying there hanging onto the phone even after he was gone, until the warning tone buzzed and made me hang it up. I lay awake the rest of the night in an agony of jealousy and regret, wondering what things he had said to her, and how he had touched her, pretending she was me. Curled in a miserable perspiring heap under the covers I touched myself, pretending it was him. And God, I thought, that was so wrong. All of it was so dishonest and unnatural and *wrong*.

The way they talked about "preserving personal integrity," all the psychologists and counselors and Dear Abbys. Vigorous group activities. Diverting natural drives into wholesome channels. They all had gray hair, how long had it been for them?

And how about it, Mother? When the guy says he loves you not before but afterward, when there is no advantage to saying it at all? And he's no evil threat to you, not a villain or some kind of playboy collecting virgins for a hobby, but only a guy? Only a guy with arms and legs and feelings and needs just like yours, somebody who's on your side? What the hell kind of a line is that, all you experts—*I love you* after another girl, slightly crocked and finally satisfied from a phone booth by the side of a highway in the rain, two counties away?

And how about me? When was I ever going to be satisfied, or didn't it matter about that? Was I just some kind of figurine in all this, some touch-me-not doll to sit safely on a shelf while he went to a stranger to get what I made him need?

Dawn came in the window and Stanley whimpered at the door, and *it's going to be all right* was what Truck had said. He had said it twice, and I could only take his word for it, whatever he meant. Whatever happened, it was going to be all right.

Chapter 8

"I think we ought to talk about the Senior Prom," Earl said that very same afternoon, waking me up from a much-needed nap with one of his friendly phone calls. On that very same phone.

Truck hadn't made it to school that day but he had come afterwards, parked and waited for me in the regular place to drive me home, and when I got in Tortoise he said, sort of grinning, "Hey, I didn't call you up last night and tell you a bunch of corny stuff, did I?" I asked him what was he going to do, take it all back now that he was sober? and he gave me this incredible look, like, *what do you think?* And I thought I might just possibly be a little bit in love, was what I thought, right there at the intersection of Parkway and Delaney. At 3:35 on a Thursday afternoon. A light turned green, a sign said "Walk," a giant hamburger with huge green plaster lettuce leaves turned slowly upon a giant pedestal and I couldn't *stand* it—I mean, just imagine. At a time like that, to have to drop me off and go pump gas all night!

I dragged upstairs, stretched out across my bed, opened my English notebook, and fell immediately asleep. The next thing I knew Earl was calling me up saying, "I think we ought to talk about the Senior Prom. Technically, we do still have a date for it, don't we?" He had asked me back in January, in a joshing and of-course-you-will manner.

Sitting up, pushing the hair out of my face, gathering what was left of my mental resources, I told Earl I felt that under the circumstances I could hardly hold him to such a date, and I naturally assumed he would take Trisha.

"Well, we've been discussing it, and Trisha says she can ask this guy Kevin who goes to Maryland who lives across the street from her. They're good friends and all. I mean, we're all mature people, we can certainly be civilized when it comes to the Senior Prom. Unless you've accepted another date, of course." Another date! Like he still had certain social options on me or something. It really ripped me off. I told him that nobody else had asked me, including Truck Hardy if that's what he was fishing for, and that if someone else should happen to ask me I would decline the invitation since I really had no desire to dress up in a formal and go to the Senior Prom.

"You have to go, Jeannie, you're on the committee."

"I'll resign from the committee, then. You're the chairman, do you want it in writing or can I just tell you over the phone?"

Earl spent the next half-hour giving me about seven hundred good reasons why I shouldn't be like that about my own Senior Prom, none of which moved me in the least. Unfortunately the subject was not closed, however, since my mother caught the essence of this conversation while delivering some freshly ironed clothes to my closet. When I confirmed that it was true, yes, I guessed I wouldn't be going to the prom this year, she sat down and wept. Actually wept. This really made me feel bad, since my mother was not at all the crying type and had never cried over anything that I had done that I could remember. Ben had drawn tears a couple of times, to be sure, but never me.

"What is this boy *doing* to you, Jeannette?" she kept sniffling. "What in the world are you letting him *do* to you?"

That was a pretty rhetorical question. I just had to wait until she had calmed down and wiped her eyes and mounted her attack in logical terms before I could start defending myself.

"He works for his money, Mother. I mean, he pumps gas and washes bird-doo off windshields for his money, and I hate to ask him to spend it on a lot of junk like tuxedoes and corsages and fifteen-dollar prom tickets."

"I never notice him running out of money to take you to the movies and buy gadgets to jazz up that car of his and drive around till all hours on school nights. Do you notice him running out of money for *those* things?"

"Oh, I know, Mother, but that's different." Here I am all prepared to argue over the Senior Prom, and already she's left the Senior Prom far behind.

"He's different all right. This boy and you are complete *opposites*. I can't imagine what you can possibly see in him, or where this is all going to *end*. Your father has always insisted on letting you and Ben make your own choices and learn your own lessons, but sooner or later *somebody* has to draw the line! Can't you see there's a difference between learning little lessons and making big *mistakes?*"

"I know, Mother—"

"You're very young, Jeannette, and I can't bear to sit back and let you drift into something you'll *regret*. All I want you to do is ask yourself where you're going before it's too *late*."

Before it's too late. That one really got me. How late was too late with a guy like Truck Hardy? First date? First kiss? First forbidden button unbuttoned?

"He respects me, if that's what you're getting at. Other girls he might do other things with, but me he respects."

"The world is full of well-respected pregnant teen-age girls, Jeannette. Do you think all teen-age fathers are *rapists?*"

"No, Mother, I don't think that." For my mother, this was pretty sensational talk. She must have been wrestling with some dark suspicions.

"If he respects you so much it seems like he could manage to take you to the Senior Prom. Or spend a few minutes visiting with your family. *Earl* was never too busy to come sit around a table and eat dinner with your family, as I recall."

"I know, Mother." I did know, of course. I knew all these things. That's the all-time worst, most annoying kind of teen-age lecture, your parents standing around telling you all these things you already know.

"You know Mother this, you know Mother that —you kids think you know everything these days. Just because men have landed on the moon that makes everything *changed,* you can throw all the old values and standards out the window. Well, let me tell you, my dear, there are some things that never change. Even in the space age, girls can still get *hurt*. And hurt in ways they might never completely *recover* from."

I didn't want to hear it, not any of it. Space age and men on the moon, little lessons and big mistakes and Senior Proms—God, they could drive you crazy. "Are you going to make me stop seeing him?" I said. "Just tell me, yes or no." Not that they could actually *make* me stop seeing him, I thought. I just wanted to know what to expect.

"Jeannette, Jeannette!" Much exasperation, more tears. "The whole point is, we have never had to make you do anything, you've always had the good sense to make yourself do the right thing. I'm not trying to be *unreasonable,* I'm only begging *you* to be reasonable.

Sit down and take a good long look at the total picture, for your own sake!"

She exited on that line, fortunately. I stared at the bright sunny LOVE! poster on the back of my closed bedroom door, doing just what she said. Taking a good long look at the total picture. I knew exactly what he was doing to me, of course, but the whole point was, it was already a little too late. I had already drifted into something, regret or no regret, and of course we were complete opposites. How else could things have been so total between us? He was the only person I had ever known who made me feel alive all over, all the time, and I could imagine very well where it would end and I just didn't care.

"I think we ought to talk about the Senior Prom," I finally said to Truck a few days later, with the dance less than a week away. I waited until a time when he was in the best of all possible moods, the big Memorial Day races out at Broom Creek, with trophies and cash prizes and even a few big contenders running from distant states like Pennsylvania and Delaware and Virginia. It was a gorgeous hot Sunday afternoon, and Tortoise was in absolute top form, and we felt so fine. Nothing but good vibrations since his phone call that night; he'd been playing it really loose and easy. No pressures, just lots of laughs. Over in the lanes the funny cars kept roaring. *"Round Two for A through E stockers,"* the guy on the loudspeaker would call out in a tinny voice that crackled all across the strip, and Truck would lean across Tortoise's engine block and kiss me on the nose or right on the mouth even, right there in the pits surrounded by dozens of guys working on their cars. It was that kind of day.

"What about the Senior Prom?"

"You hadn't thought of asking me or anything, had you?"

"I was sort of hoping somebody else would."

"I don't really want to go either, Bubba, but the thing is, all of a sudden it's a big family crisis if Jeannie doesn't go to the Senior Prom. My parents think you don't respect me." He rolled his eyes up toward the blue and cloudless sky. "I know, I know, but I'm going to hear a lot less grief about it if we go. It can be my treat, no kidding. Since I asked you to it, I really want to pay for everything."

"Oh, forget about the money, I don't care about the money. I just can't stand the thought of putting on one of those monkey suits."

"You could wear a regular suit, maybe. Just don't wear your cowboy boots, and you can get by with it."

"With everybody else in a monkey suit? You kidding? It's not bad enough I dance like a three-legged mule, I have to show up looking like the janitor too?"

"Maybe you ought to wear a monkey suit."

"Modified Production entries to staging lanes Three and Four," the announcer droned out.

"All right," Truck said. "I'll do it, I'll rent me a money suit. I'll even get my sideburns trimmed. If that's not respect—man. I might go down in history as the first guy to ever die of respecting a girl." And he banged down the hood and pinched me in a very disrespectful spot and went for another run.

Tortoise was magnificent all the way through the class competition that afternoon. In the first round he beat a '68 GTO with no sweat, and won the second by default when a '56 Ford jumped too soon and redlighted. In the third and fourth he beat a pair of Corvettes, one by a little and the other by a lot, until in the late-afternoon final round, after about a million other gassers and dragsters and funny cars and streetables and beat-up pickups in a thousand other classes ran, it came down to Truck and one other guy in a '55 Chevy for the class trophy.

"You know who that guy is?" he said nonchalantly,

tightening a little bolt that did not look at all like it needed tightening. "That's Jimmy Terrell."

"Wow," I said. I didn't know Jimmy Terrell from a hole in the ground, a fact Truck was well aware of. He gave me a very level look.

"I don't quite know how to break this to you, but I think he might beat me out there. I mean, the odds on that are very good, considering he turned in an 11:45 on his last run."

"In that little old blue car?"

"That little old blue car just happened to win the class trophy at the Nationals last year. That's the *Nationals*. Like, fastest car in this class in the nation."

"Wow." I looked at Terrell a little closer.

"So, you gonna put me down and run off with Terrell tonight if he wins?"

"You bet I am. He's a real doll." He was skinny as a post and had a high, ducktailed pompadour and a gigantic Adam's apple.

"Hear that, Tortoise? We might unload her yet! Hey." Hand around the back of my neck. "One little kiss for luck." Then the speaker was crackling out last call, and he was gone.

They moved down into the staging lanes and finally to the starting line, Truck in Lane One with Jimmy Terrell *vroom-vrooming* in Lane Two. I looked at Tortoise's shiny sides, all black and white and chrome, and I loved that car, I really did. He looked so brave and chipper, just like a salty little old man with headlights for eyes and a Chevy-V nose and wide grimacing grille, and the guardian angel swinging like a pendant, watching over all. I swear, sometimes I think I could love any creature under the sun I took the trouble to get to know.

I don't care, I kept telling myself, *let him lose, if he loses I'll love him even more, I'll love him if he redlights, I'll love him if he blows a shift*—standing there practically having heart failure waiting for the lights to blink down to Go.

On green Terrell surged forward in a terrific burst but Truck came up smooth right behind him, gaining fast and steady, moving in so close at the finish line that I couldn't tell who crossed first until they had cruised past and up over the hill and the win light started flashing over Lane One.

Lane One!

Of all the many moments in my seventeen-year existence, that had to be the highest. I squealed out something untranslatable and my soul utterly split from my body and floated free—with me following behind as fast as my tough-looking legs could go, running down the fence and across the pits to the return road. I ran right in front of him, made him stop and let me in the car. He didn't know he had won. It was so close he didn't know until he saw me and then all he could say was "Oh, baby!" over and over. I didn't know if he meant *oh, baby* me or *oh, baby* the car, but it didn't matter—Tortoise was golden. Good old Tortoise, he did it just for us!

The guy handed him his E.T. card and the trophy card, and he took it up to Pop Summers in the tower and exchanged it for the little gold trophy cup, which he handed right over to me. Kissing me on the eyebrow, ear lobe, and mouth despite the fact that all these guys are coming around congratulating him. Even Jimmy Terrell came up and shook his hand, and some guy in the background kept saying "Kee-rist, did you catch that E.T.? *Eleven forty-three!*"

"That a new track record?"

"*Track* record—that's a *record* record, period!"

"You're hot today, Hardy!" Pop said. "You want to take these fifty bills in cash right now, or stick around for the eliminations and triple it?"

Truck thought it over for a minute, looked at the ground and looked at the trophy and looked at Tortoise and finally said no, he thought he'd pushed the old boy hard enough for one day. "Think I'm gonna leave 'em clapping in the stands this time, Pop. Quit while I'm winning."

Which couldn't have pleased me more, since *I* sure didn't feel much like sticking around for the eliminations. I didn't know exactly what I wanted to do, but not stick around for the eliminations.

What we ended up doing was driving around the county until we found a little combination grocery store and gas station open, where we bought some bread and ham and cheese. On one side there was a dairy case with chilled beer and wine.

"Oh, champagne," I said. "Let's get some champagne."

"Not on Sunday," the old guy said, clicking his false teeth. "We got blue laws around here, you know."

"We won't tell anybody."

"Sorry, I just can't sell it to you."

Truck looked at me and then looked at the guy and said, "How about if I steal it? And happen to lose five dollars as I'm going out the door?"

"I don't want no trouble, sonny."

"How about if I happen to lose ten dollars as I'm going out the door?"

The old guy looked down at the counter and just clicked his false teeth. Truck opened the dairy case and handed me a cool bottle, green with gold foil, and left a folded-up bill in its place.

"How are we going to open it?" I said as we turned off the highway onto a narrow dirt road through a pasture, but he had that figured too. From the glove compartment he produced a fantastic pocketknife that had about sixty-five different attachments including a corkscrew. From the trunk he produced a blanket. We parked Tortoise and squeezed through a broken fence into a field marked "No Trespassing."

"Forgive us our trespasses," I intoned. "As we forgive those who trespass against us."

"Amen, sister, a-*men*." He spread the blanket out under a willow tree, popped the cork up into the branches and we drank a long bubbly toast to Tortoise, sitting there in the middle of somebody's field. We drank it right out of his trophy cup, he from one side and I from the other.

"I knew these little mothers must be good for something," he said.

The sun was rapidly going down but we were 'way up there, really sailing, and what did we need with champagne when we were already so high on the day and the air and each other? The bottle was still more than half full when I took it out of his hands and leaned it carefully against the tree and hugged him, just hugged him for all I was worth.

"Careful, I break easy," he kept groaning, lying back against the blanket letting me kiss him, but I didn't want to be careful, I wanted to keep going until something broke between us. Things couldn't keep going up and up forever. Somewhere something had to give way.

After a while he pulled the blanket up over my shoulders and dusk was falling all around us, no lights anywhere and nobody else for miles, only the two of us. And then even we were going to be one, we knew it at the same moment. Because for once everything was equal between us; he knew I loved him and I knew he loved me and we simply couldn't stop. I couldn't stop and he couldn't stop and if it was immoral let it be immoral, I didn't care. Nothing could be as immoral as leaving each other aching and frustrated when peace was so close, and so natural, and so right.

And if not exactly right for me, it was at least right for him, I knew, when the breath went out of him all at once and he kissed my neck and lay still. *That was it,* I thought slowly, *I'm a woman now,* and I tried to feel happy and good over it but I could only feel strange. It was like he wasn't even there any more. He'd left me far behind somewhere and the ground suddenly felt very hard.

He didn't say anything for the longest time, just lit a cigarette and sat back against the tree with his eyes closed and finally he looked at me a little sheepishly and said, "Should've brought that guardian angel along."

"Pardon?"

"What I mean is, I don't think the world is quite ready for a little Truck Hardy Junior yet."

"Oh. Yes, well, I think it's all right." My mind groped over the old monthly business, safe days and danger days. "I'm due in about a week." Prom day, I thought dully. Or probably the day after.

"Then it's all right," he said. Big expert, naturally.

The drive home seemed terribly long, much longer than the drive out there.

"I didn't hurt you too much, did I?" he said when we had gone about ten or fifteen miles. I told him not too much, I thought I would live. I was trying to smile and pass it off lightly, but he just kept on. "I guess it wasn't very good for you, was it?"

I really didn't feel much like discussing it.

"I promise," he said, "I'll make it better for you next time. And I'll use something a little safer than the guardian angel."

"Next time?" I said faintly. "Please. Let's not start talking about next time."

"Come on, now." Reaching over, taking my hand. "You think this changes the way I feel about you, don't you? You females and your respect! I'm telling you, it doesn't change a thing."

We females and *our* respect.

"Look, Bubba, can't we worry about it later?"

It would probably be better, I decided, thinking it out very carefully, if I just made sure I didn't let it happen again. The fact that it wasn't very good for me made it like I was still a virgin anyway, practically. I had learned a lesson, that's all. I knew what it was like now, I wouldn't be curious about it any more. I was probably even better off for it. The main thing was my own attitude, the way I thought of myself for it, and it was just a natural thing that could happen to anybody under circumstances like those.

"What did you do with that bread and ham and stuff?" he said.

"It's down here, still in the sack."

"Why don't you fix us a couple of sandwiches? Make mine, like, bread, ham, cheese, ham, cheese, ham, bread. Man, I am really starved. All that changing tires and driving and all, that'll do it to you. Aren't you hungry?"

"No," I said, "I guess it's the champagne or something." But it wasn't the champagne that was making me sick, it was him, this drag racer with sideburns and a Southern accent driving his stupid souped-up car with one hand and eating a big fat sandwich with the other, talking with his mouth full like nothing had happened—about how much it was going to help him, beating Terrell like that today, with reporters from the drag magazines there seeing Tortoise turn in an 11.43.

"Hey, look," he said on my front porch when we were finally, blessedly home. "What we did, it's no big deal. You know? People do it every day. Doesn't matter to me, one way or the other. Nobody's forcing you to do nothing. You want me to get lost, I'll get lost. It's up to you."

"No, Truck, I don't want you to get lost." Wow, that was all I needed. To have Truck Hardy do a thing like that to me and then casually pick up and go.

"I mean, goddamn. I wish it hadn't happened, if that's the way you feel. I thought you wanted it, but O.K. All right. Whatever you say."

"Now you're mad."

"No, I'm not mad."

"Then come in for just a minute."

"I can't. I told you, I got this term paper that was due last Friday. I'll flunk out for sure if I don't hand it in."

"All right," I said, "if you have to go home, then go on home." I wanted to die. "So long."

"Do you think I could maybe have one lousy little good-night kiss or something?"

"Oh, Bubba." He made me want to laugh and cry and die all at the same time, and I couldn't stand it. He gave me one little kiss that wasn't a bit lousy, then he left.

I stood on the porch and watched till Tortoise's taillights were out of sight and then went upstairs and took a long soaking bath with bubbles right up to my neck. The longer I lay there, the more I had to admit that it really hadn't been his fault, he always had left it up to me, and I believed him when he said he would in the future. That made me feel a lot better, to know I still had that choice. It was just something that had happened, that's all. Something that might, but then again might not, ever happen again.

Monday there was no school, and Truck was working all day to make up for time he had missed over the weekend, so I took Trisha out to our club for opening day of the pool. It turned out to be a very entertaining scene, warm and chlorinated and bright bluegreen. Trisha spent the whole afternoon flirting with the new long-haired lifeguards, who flirted right back, and I came home tired and sunburned and feeling fairly mellow about things. Like there was nothing really so tragic about losing one's virginity, it was something that happened to everybody sooner or later. Like getting born and growing old and dying. In a certain crazy sense, it almost made a girl freer. Because she wasn't just a little girl after that, she was free to go either way.

Not that I planned on making a habit of it, or anything. It was just that things could have been a lot worse.

Chapter 9

That week was Senior Week, which meant Senior Slump in its most blatant and undiluted form: all us short-timers floating in and out of class and riding around in convertibles and just generally making the rest of Albemarle High School glad that we would soon be moving on. I didn't see much of Truck at school, he skipped a couple of days and worked a few extra late shifts, but he did call me up and chat for a while every night. And I was fairly busy myself, with so many other diverting things going on.

I spent all day Saturday down at the hotel, helping with the "Love and Peace" table decorations and last-minute prom arrangements. Because of a couple of minor emergencies, like nobody could locate where the management had stored the boxes of little stuffed-dove favors, I was late getting home and getting ready, and I kept poor Truck waiting downstairs in my living room for an outrageously long time.

At one point my mother came up to check on my progress. She fussed around with some wisps of my hair for a minute and then said in this stoic, defeated voice, "He looks very nice, Jeannette." That really killed me. I thought I looked pretty nice, too. My dress was long and simple and graceful, yellow dotted swiss with a low scooped neckline. I'd told Truck not to bother with flowers, since I had them for my hair, the front pulled back and tied on top with a tiny cluster of something white and sweet that I didn't know the name of.

And oh, did he ever look nice. It was almost comical for Truck Hardy to come on in a tuxedo looking like the Beautiful People. Trousers crisp, shirt smooth and starched, every stud and cuff link perfectly in place.

"Don't forget, we're going to that breakfast at Patty's afterwards, so don't wait up," I told my parents. They didn't look too happy about it, but it was an ancient Albemarle tradition, all-night hell-raising proms.

"What's that about breakfast?" Truck said after we got in Tortoise. He didn't look so terribly happy himself.

"You know, after the prom everybody drags over to somebody's house for something to eat. Just to keep things going. Patty invited me. You too, of course. She's a friend of mine. We don't have to stay too long."

"Oh."

"Is something the matter?"

"No."

But something was the matter, very definitely. I thought maybe it was the monkey suit, or the fact that he had to wait so long chatting with my parents, or maybe just the idea of the Senior Prom being so much my scene. He could be so damn egotistical about things.

"Did you get your little friend today?" he said after a while. "You know."

"Not today, probably tomorrow." So then I thought maybe that's what was on his mind.

I didn't find out until much later what was really bugging him. Even then, he tried to shrug it off. "I'm just not graduating, that's all. It's that bitch Strickland, naturally. Say look, you think this hotel has any ashtrays? You're a big wheel around here, maybe you could pull some strings and get me one."

"What do you mean, not graduating? How can you not be graduating? How long have you known?" I went over and got him an ashtray.

"Well, you know that term paper. She decided to make a big deal out of it, let it count as the whole grade for the last six weeks. She's so lazy, she figured that way she wouldn't have to grade a whole bunch of papers. Just one shot, all or nothing. It could be about anything we wanted, she said, as long as it had something to do with English. Then she handed out this list with about fifteen rules and sources and junk you were supposed to have in the paper. I took one look at it and knew there was no way I was going to be able to write this paper doing all that stuff, so I just figured screw the list, and sat down and wrote my paper out of my head. You know how everybody writes papers like that, Jeannie. They get books out of the library and copy a little bit out of each book and change the words around and don't even know what the hell their paper says."

"So what did you write on?"

"You know when we were talking that day about *Romeo and Juliet,* how you said seeing the movie wasn't as good as reading it and studying the footnotes and everything? Well, I said just the opposite in my paper. Like how if you didn't get the feel of something it didn't do you any good at all, and you couldn't get it by reading the same way as seeing it acted out in front of you. And I used all these examples and everything."

"Didn't she like it?"

"She asked me what was my source for all that stuff and I said nothing, I just wrote it. So she whipped out her goddamn list of rules and said that made it only my opinion then, and it said clearly that this was not an opinion term paper, but a research term paper. And

I was supposed to use at least three books or magazines, and there was a lot of stuff I could find written on that subject, if I'd look in this certain file in the library. Plus I didn't do it on one side of the paper in typewriter or ink and check it over for spelling errors, like the list said, and finally she said she just wasn't going to accept it that way. She said the general idea of it was all right, but if I wanted it to count I'd have to do it over and do it by the rules this time. And the way it worked out, I was right on the border between passing and flunking, and if I flunked her course I wouldn't graduate, because you can't graduate if you flunk English, so she said I better think it over real careful about doing this paper right. She wanted me to kiss her butt, is what she wanted me to do. I been giving her a pretty hard time all semester, so she had me where she wanted me and she was pretty happy about it, too. She thought she was going to see me crawl. I told her to take her goddamn list of rules and cram it."

"Oh, Bubba." I stared across the table at him in absolute despair. "How could you do that? Throw away twelve years of school just like that? You've got to at least get a high school diploma, you are never ever going to be able to do anything without a high school diploma!"

"The hell I can't. I've got a driver's license and a good pair of hands, that's all I need."

"But that's so stupid, Truck—to fight it out for so long and then let it drop like that, with three weeks to go! Just because of a little—pride!"

"Okay, Teach, I'm proud and stupid—now that we got that straight, you want to go home? I mean, I wouldn't want you to be embarrassed, your friends seeing you at the Senior Prom with some proud and stupid guy dressed up in a monkey suit."

"Look, Bubba, I didn't mean it that way, so don't— oh, never mind. I'll tell you what. I'll help you with the paper, O.K.? Go tell Strickland you changed your mind. You'll be out soon and you'll never have to see her again, what do you care about your pride? And I can start looking through the vertical file, I know how to find the articles. They have a lot of film magazines and English journals in the library—"

He just sat there and waited for me to finish. "Does it really matter that much to you, Jeannie? A *diploma*? It's a piece of paper with fancy writing on it. You gonna marry me if I get it and not marry me if I don't?"

I surrendered my case to him then, realizing in some part of my head deeper than reason that he was righter than Strickland, and wiser than me, and much truer to himself than anyone I had ever known. And that if he ended up suffering for it he wouldn't be the first person to suffer for being true to himself. And that if there was anything to be learned here, it was me who should be doing the learning. All of this hitting me at once in a way I found impossible to understand fully, much less translate into words to answer him.

The band was playing a rare slow number so I said, "This is a dance, Bubba, why don't we dance?"

"I can't dance, you know how I dance. I dance about the same way you fish."

At that point, it seemed the best thing I could do was go to the ladies' lounge. When I returned a few minutes later, outrage of outrages, he was dancing with Trisha Sewall.

"Don't I know you from somewhere?" I said to Earl, who was sitting at a table looking on blankly.

"What is it about that guy, anyway?"

"Don't worry about it, Earl. It will probably be a good experience for her. Very educational," I said, and went to retrieve my date the minute the song had ended.

"Not much you can't dance, you just looked like Arthur Murray out there, that's all."

"Wasn't my idea, she asked me. She said I looked

lonesome." Green-eyed innocence, of all things. "Do you think I look lonesome? Or is it more like proud and stupid? If you want to know what I think, I think I look like a jackass. I think we ought to go."

Believe it or not, things got even worse. Just about that time Wally and Mac and Ray with their lovely ladies decided to make a surprise entrance, dressed like Hell's Angels and smelling like a brewery. Naturally, Truck was the first person they wanted to look up, "to see if he's really for real, man." By the time the chaperones finally got them to leave, Truck's usual cool had been blown to shreds and it was all I could do to keep up with his long strides through the plush marble lobby.

He made the half-hour run from the hotel to my house in about sixteen minutes and pulled up in front with a very final jerk. "What do you say we just can the whole thing, Jeannie—you and me. Just shake hands and call it a draw."

"No," I protested. "I say, no."

"You don't wanna go where I'm going, I guarantee it. Not now, not tomorrow, not ever. No way."

"Yes, I do."

"I'm going straight from here to the falls and throw every bit of these frills into the water and then jump right in myself."

"Then I want to go watch."

"I believe it."

"I *love* you," I said finally, one last desperation try. "Love. You. Really."

"Oh, Christ." He collapsed briefly over the steering wheel. "You love me. Man, I'm glad you love me. Can you imagine what life would be like if you *didn't* love me?"

But that seemed to make a difference. He stopped fighting it after that. Gave up and put Tortoise in gear and drove us away again, luckily without attracting the attention of my parents.

Once Truck and I had cut school and gone to the falls and spent a whole afternoon climbing on the rocks. It was great fun at the time, jumping over crevasses and scaling sheer rock walls and teetering over the water where a slipped foot could have meant instant *zap*. The place was closed at night, of course, with signs that said "Paths Closed After Sunset" by order of the National Park Commission, but they were low signs. You could easily step over them. And they didn't exactly patrol the place after dark, it was so mammoth—acres and acres of boulders, with water shooting down narrow chasms spanned by wooden bridges, all the way to the river. And on the edge of a cliff was a platform overlooking the big falls themselves, where the wide expanse of river fell into an incredible tumult of rapids, foaming and churning, filling the air with a low steady roar.

There was a little moon up over the water that night, nothing too spectacular, but enough so I could see the expression on his face, which was still far from contented.

"O.K., you came for the show, here goes the show," he said, and took off the studs and threw them as far as he could, one at a time. It was like a little game, Truck Hardy Throwing the Gold-Plated Stud Across the Potomac. Next the cuff links, one at a time, and then the bow tie, and finally the cummerbund. I wondered if the tux rental place made allowances for people who got mad and threw their stuff in the river.

"Just for the record, Teach, you're the first girl that ever got me into one of these mothers, and so help me, you're gonna be the last."

He didn't say anything else for a while, just stood there looking over the railing with his shirt flapping around his neck and wrists, and finally he said, "You know where I went this morning? I went down and talked to the Marine recruiter."

"Oh, Bubba." The mere word Marine was enough to fill me with dread.

"When I was a kid I always kind of wanted to be one of those guys who parachute out of planes."

"Into minefields? Carrying machine guns and nerve gas? To get blown up or blow up somebody else—"

"Relax, Teach, I didn't sign up. Nothing proud and stupid like that. I just bulled with them for a while, and after that I drove up to Frederick County and talked to Pop some."

"What did he say?"

"About the same thing you did. Something real sweet like, if I was his kid he'd beat my little dropout ass for a dumb move like that. Christ, what is it about me, anyway? Fifty thousand things I can do and none of them are the things that count. Then as soon as there's one stupid little thing I can't handle, that's it, baby. That's the key to the whole ball game."

He went on like that for a long time—about why it was ridiculous, this thing with me and him, and why we really ought to just can it. About all the things he had been and hadn't been, might possibly be and could never be, wanted to be and didn't want to be. About Tennessee and West Virginia, his old man and his old lady and more schools than he could count, bourbon bottles and broken-up farms and poker chips for toys.

"Ah, the hell with it," he said finally. "You wonder why I feel like joining the Marines and putting twelve thousand miles between me and this place?"

"I wish you'd stop saying that."

"Why? I might as well be twelve thousand miles from here right now. Twelve thousand miles from the snotty halls of Albemarle High School. Especially twelve thousand miles from *you*. I mean, what am I supposed to do, anyway—just stand around and pump gas and hold your hand until graduation? What about

July and August? What about September? Huh? Tell me about September."

"I don't want to talk about September right now, Truck. This is only June, and it so happens I'm freezing." I really was cold, my arms and shoulders were very bare and the spray blew across the falls and I was standing there with my arms folded and my teeth chattering.

He let out a long breath, and took off the forlornly flapping shirt. "Why didn't you say something?"

"It seemed kind of trivial."

"*Trivial?* Oh, man. You and your fifty-cent words! You gotta remember now, I'm just a high school dropout."

But he draped the shirt around my shoulders and held me to him for a minute and it was all right again, he was so warm, and the bitterness was all out and gone.

He had on a T-shirt with "Crane Racing Cams" on it underneath the elegant white dress shirt, and I said, "Crane racing cams?"

"Damn right, Crane racing cams. The best made."

We went back to the car then, crossing back over the rickety bridges above the rushing torrents. He walked with his arm around me so I wouldn't be dizzy, and I had never felt so close to another human being in all my life. I knew exactly what was going to happen and I didn't care, I was crazy to think it could ever be any other way with us now.

When we reached Tortoise he got the blanket out of the trunk and folded it around my head and shoulders Indian-style and said, now, was that warm enough? I pressed my face against his Crane racing cams T-shirt and he didn't play around with me any, he just came right out and asked would I let him make love to me again? He knew what I said before but he couldn't help it, he just wanted me to know how it could be when it was right. God knows, he said, he could do that, even if he couldn't pass English, he could make love good for me if I would only let him. I didn't say anything, just stood there quietly blowing my mind, and by the time he finally got around to kissing me I didn't need to say anything; it would've taken a seismograph to measure what was going on between us.

The blanket was the same blanket as before, but the back seat of the car turned out to be a lot softer than the ground, and, sure enough, he didn't leave me behind this trip. He took me right with him every slow step of the way, with a thousand kisses and touches and whispered questions, all the things he hadn't taken the trouble to do before. No hesitations, nothing held back—just *here I am, all of me, there you are, all of you*—giving and taking all fused into one single motion until it was impossible to tell where my pleasure left off and his began.

"Oh, Jeannie," he said at last, and his voice was soft and deep in his throat. He wasn't so nonchalant about it afterward this time. "Baby. I'm not believing that one." And I wasn't believing it either, that body and mind could ever be so together that way. That it had been there all this time, just waiting for me.

He kissed me once more and we couldn't move, we were so wrecked, so far out of ourselves, totally crashed. *I could die right now*, I thought, *and I wouldn't regret all those unlived older years*. But of course I wasn't about to die; teen-age lovers never die in real life. They just occasionally get lucky at making the world go away.

We went to sleep together, but he woke up first because when I came to sometime right before dawn, things just getting gray outside, he was lying there looking at me.

"Wake up, little Susie," he grinned.

"Ohhh. Bubba." Dress crumpled, flowers wilted, mascara everywhere.

"You sure you don't want to talk about September?"

September. I shook my head helplessly. To even think of talking about September, after that night.

"If you think I'm gonna do that paper over for Strickland on account of you, you're crazy."

Strickland. Boy, was he wide awake. I looked in the mirror and started giggling, of all things. For a minute I wondered if maybe I was getting hysterical, but then I stopped.

"I think you're crazy anyhow, you know that?" He leaned across the seat and turned on the radio, just in time to hear one of Country Carl Barton's early-morning colleagues inform us it was 5:47 A.M.

"Reckon we missed that breakfast?" he said as we began to make haste with zippers and suspenders, hooks and eyes, combs and Kleenex. Like an old silent-comedy routine, funny but not so funny, demonstrating this obnoxious habit the world has of coming back in the morning.

Chapter 10

Mr. Gunther, the principal, called me into his office about a week before graduation. *He knows,* I thought. *How could he possibly know?* On his desk was a calendar with Snoopy lying on top of his doghouse. To think that I had put such confidence in a calendar, as though calendars were sacred or something.

"How have you been doing, Jeannette?" he asked in his friendly booming voice.

Well, sir, I've gone to bed with L. P. Hardy a few times. Not actually in bed, of course. People just say "go to bed" because it sounds nicer than a few of the other ways of saying it. I myself like to think of it as making love. I don't know how L. P. Hardy likes to think of it. Except when we're actually doing it, I don't really believe he thinks much about it at all.

"Fine, Mr. Gunther," I said. "It isn't long now till the big day, is it?"

"Well, Jeannette, that's what I wanted to see you about. We've run into a slight emergency with the graduation program. I'm sure you're aware that the major student speaker is traditionally the class president, but Ron Lewis has just come down with mononucleosis, it seems. Even if he feels able to attend the ceremonies, of course, he won't be up to making a major address. Since you're the vice president, we were hoping you would agree to take his place. I realize this is awfully short notice, but you've always had a lot of poise and stage presence, so to speak, and we think you would make a fine contribution."

This was the type of thing that nearly cracked me up. With Hester Prynne at least it was out in the open, she had to wear the letter A for adultery across her breast. Sometimes I felt so hypocritical that I wondered if I wouldn't feel better wearing a sign myself, some scarlet letters saying *She Does It With Truck Hardy. And Likes It, Too.*

At first I thought Truck might tell. I begged him not to and he gave his word he wouldn't, but you never know. In the parking lot or at the drive-in somebody might say, "Hey, Hardy, you got her yet?" And he would say, "Hell no, man, she got *me*." Or maybe he would just smile. That's all it would take, really. Then everybody would know but he wouldn't have told them, see, so it wouldn't be like he had gone back on his word. He was very serious about people keeping their word.

At the drugstore one day I looked over the different brands of contraceptive foam. I didn't buy any because I didn't know where I would keep it so my mother wouldn't find it, and anyway, after those first two times Truck started using rubbers. He kept them in a box in the glove compartment of the car. It was kind of awkward and unspontaneous that way, but then you can't have everything. But at the drugstore that day I thought, supposing he was irresponsible and left that sort of thing up to me, what precautions would I take? There was this one brand that had proved ninety-six percent effective, the box said, when used as directed. All I could do was wonder about that other four percent. As long as there was a four-percent possibility of error, they may as well have said, this stuff doesn't work at all. The Four Percent would be a good name for a musical group, I thought. An all-girl band at a home for unwed mothers. And now the Four Percent, all single, singing their latest hit single, "Lost Along the Way." That may sound funny, but it wasn't really all that funny. Actually the whole thing made me feel a little sick. That wouldn't be morning sickness already, because I was only a couple of weeks overdue, but it was just that I had been so sure about that exact day, and now I couldn't remember why I had been so sure.

Also it was possible I might have VD and not even know it. There is one kind in three stages where it flares up in the first stage and then goes away. It doesn't really go away, that's just the second stage. It lies dormant in your body for a long time and then the eggs hatch. They hatch into worms which travel through your bloodstream to your brain and eat your brain. People used to die of this kind all the time in the eighteenth century. I would sit in class wondering if you could feel these worms in your brain or if your brain had pain nerves. I had no idea who else Truck might have been doing it with. One of these girls might have had VD and he wouldn't know it and then he would pass it on to me.

I knew he would never do this purposely, but many people hurt other people without meaning to. They also hurt themselves sometimes without realizing what they are doing. I thought about people who take LSD and things like that without realizing that their minds aren't strong enough to take the mental shock of these drugs, then they become psychotic and have to be hospitalized. They were just experimenting around, they didn't know until after they did it that it wasn't the right thing for them, considering their particular mind and all, but by then it's too late. They're already on a bad trip and there's no return road.

I also began to write poetry. In class, at home, everywhere. In English class we were studying this poem by an English poet about the Trojan War and Helen of Troy. You may remember her as the face that launched a thousand ships—the unfaithful Greek queen who took a bad trip with the Trojan prince Paris, who certainly looked attractive enough at the time. This story of the Trojan War was the first known story recorded in Western literature, our English teacher said, nearly 2800 years ago. Everybody wrote that down in their notebooks. *1st kn. stry. rcded. in W. lit. 2800 yrs. ago.* I thought how ironic it was, that the first known story recorded in Western literature nearly 2800 years ago all began with a lady who let herself drift into something she would regret. I tried to picture how she felt and in trig class one day. I wrote a poem in the back of my history notebook that went like this:

> She stands on the city wall
> And looks back across the land
> The way she came,
> Forgetting why she came.
> She could go home perhaps,
> But home wouldn't be the same.
> There would always be a part of Troy
> Left in her, she would never be able
> To wash herself clean of the boy.

Bad poetry, but it was a good outlet. And I really sort of needed an outlet. There was nobody I could talk to, certainly not Earl or Trisha. My other friends were impossibly remote, and naturally, when I really needed Ben, he would be late coming home from college. As for my parents, I knew they must be concerned about my strange frame of mind around the house, but I didn't want to hurt them. You don't usually tell your parents about something like that anyway, unless you are pregnant and have to tell them, but only if you have to. You wouldn't want to blow it by saying anything before you knew for sure, because what if it turned out you were just a few weeks late with your period? Then you'd have spilled the whole thing all for nothing, and they would surely make you stop seeing the guy, and then where would you be?

My mother kept casually bringing up the subject of Earl Corbett. She had liked it so much when he hung around the kitchen and joked with her and stayed for dinner. She was hoping we would get back together again eventually, I could tell. Once she said, "You know, Jeannette, when two people have problems the very best thing is to sit down face to face and talk it out, not let it go on too long." She thought I kept dating Truck to make Earl jealous because Earl was dating Trisha to make me jealous. "Lord," she said, "I remember once your father and I had a fight that lasted three months! We didn't speak to each other for three months, and made ourselves miserable when it was really a silly misunderstanding that would have been cleared up right away if we had only given in and had a good heart-to-heart talk."

I wondered if my mother and my father had ever done it before they were married.

At the time of this conversation we were shopping for curtains and bedspreads for my dorm room at Darcey next fall. My mother said she saw no point in waiting till later in the summer to do this shopping, because by then everything would be picked over. The dorm room I was assigned was pink, the letter from the Office of Residences said. My roommate was Brenda Newman, from Richmond, Virginia. I could write her, but I hardly knew what to say. *Dear Brenda, How are you? I am fine. Well, not fine really. Do you have a boyfriend? I have this boy I'm rather deeply involved with, probably not the sort of person I would end up marrying, though, in fact, you'd probably never guess by looking at him and then at me that we . . .*

I thought I would wait instead and let her write me

first. She had my address, too. Let her write me first.

The bedspreads we picked out were brown-and-white striped. Actually my mother was the one who picked them out. She said she thought that would blend well with any shade of pink, since we didn't know if it was light pink or dark pink or more on the order of mauve. "Maybe Brenda will bring a rug or some pictures," she said.

I wondered if Brenda Newman had ever done it with a boy.

"Have you got any questions?" Mr. Gunther said. "Be glad to help you out in any way."

Well, sir, I could use some help in figuring out what to do if this thing should turn out to be true. As far as morals go, I believe it is more sinful to bring a child into the world unwanted than to have an abortion, but that's just my personal view. I wouldn't want to go to one of these coat-hanger places, though, because I know there are places you can go now that are safe and legal, I'm just not sure where these places are or how to go about it. Of course, it's too soon at this point even to go to a regular doctor to find out, so I suppose there's still a little time to look into all the alternatives.

"Why do they call it commencement?" I asked him.

"Pardon?"

"Graduation. I always wondered why they call it commencement, when it seems like more of an ending."

"Well, Jeannette, the idea is that it's the beginning of your adult life, I believe. You're getting ready to enter a new world, commence a new life. That would make a good topic for your address. Why don't you work on it?"

I thanked him and told him I would. Actually I thought it was a terrible topic for a commencement address. I thought everyone in the country who gave a commencement speech probably spoke on the topic of commencement marking the beginning of a new life.

Truck was not coming to school any more, of course, but I still saw him at night. I didn't tell my parents he had dropped out because I was afraid that would be the last straw and they wouldn't let me see him at all any more. Once or twice, in especially nervous moments, I felt that I truly didn't want to see him any more. Once I thought I was going to scream if he kissed me one more time. But mostly, I wanted to see him more than ever. And I was sort of glad when he began working early shifts during the daytime so he could be with me more at night. Because although he was the problem, he was also the only comfort.

He said not to worry, if it happened it just happened, that's all, and he would marry me. We would make the best of it, he said. I told him I thought that would be a bad thing to do, much better simply not to have the baby.

"I don't know about that," he said. "If there's a baby in there it's partly my baby too, and I'm not so sure I want anybody killing any baby of mine."

This little irrational, egotistical streak of his had once seemed so amusing to me, when nothing was serious and nothing mattered, but everything mattered now, and nothing was amusing any more. Not even the drag racing. The drag racing was still a fun thing and a harmless thing and even a wholesome thing, of course, but not the kind of thing to build a life around, when you got right down to it. I mean, trying to see how fast a car could go down a quarter-mile track. For him, maybe. But for me?

Gradually I formed a very realistic vision of what life with him would really be—possibly the only realistic vision I had ever had. An easygoing treadmill of trailers and campgrounds and racetracks and beer joints, attractive from a distance, but not so satisfactory after you'd been there a while. A nice place to visit, in other words. Or cheap apartments with fake chandeliers.

Baby and then more babies, fistfights and lovemaking, nothing ever above the level of paychecks and paperbacks, and little chance of change. I wanted an education, but how would I ever get an education? I wanted to be a teacher, and I would never be a teacher.

Sometimes when we were out driving I thought that if I could jump out of the car perhaps the blow would make me have a miscarriage, but then he never drove recklessly or even fast any more. I think he was always thinking about the possibility of the baby. It filled me with such panic when I finally began to suspect that Truck Hardy actually wanted me to have his baby. He never admitted it, of course. He never did come right out and say he was against the abortion idea because he wanted us to be married, but I thought surely he must feel that way from the way he acted, and it gave me a terrible trapped feeling. It was hard to believe that he was the same person who had once made me feel so free.

Once when I was thirteen I read this book about a home for unwed mothers. It said a lot of the girls had boyfriends waiting to marry them after it was all over. These boyfriends weren't the fathers of their babies, though, the fathers of their babies were actually other boys that these girls decided they did not want to marry and live with for the rest of their lives. How could that be possible? I wondered when I read this book. How could a girl do it with somebody she did not care enough about to marry? The guy would have to be a complete beast, I thought, who never gave the girl a chance. That shows how much I knew when I was thirteen.

It wasn't that I didn't care about him as much, it was just that I was suddenly able to see him for what he really was instead of what I wanted him to be. He was a nineteen-year-old boy, a person of many minor potentials but few major prospects. Proud and stubborn and foolish, but kind and clever and very strong, in his own way. A fine friend and a very good lover. But still a nineteen-year-old boy.

I'd never been too religious but we did belong to a church and so in June one Sunday I went to church. I listened to the organ play "Praise God from whom all blessings flow, praise him all creatures here below," but I didn't sing because I was afraid I would begin crying. I had come by myself, but there were a few people around me that I knew and I didn't want them to see me crying in church. So I looked at the stained-glass windows all around and the big one in the middle that had etched into the glass, "Repent and Ye Shall Be Saved."

I certainly needed to be saved, but I did not know exactly what to repent of, because I wasn't sure what part of what we had done together was immoral. I knew that "Thou shalt not commit adultery" was one of the Ten Commandments, of course. But then the Bible went on to say that to look at a guy and even think about doing it with him was as bad as actually doing it, which I thought sort of ruined the forcefulness of the original commandment. Like if you did the one you might as well go ahead and do the other, that's what it implied.

In fact, I began to think it was a little absurd for people to believe things had to be so, just because they were written in a particular book. If there was one thing Truck Hardy had taught me, it was to be a little less worshipful of books just because they were books. It was my own personal opinion anyway that no book could come right out and say it was immoral to make love to somebody, period, that's it, subject closed. What Truck and I had done seemed to have been more foolish and careless than immoral, really. So I tried that for a while, looking at the stained-glass window and repenting for having been foolish and careless, but somehow that didn't feel right. I didn't think that was quite what they meant by "Repent and Ye Shall Be Saved."

So in the end I just repented for everything, everything I could think of that I had done, including skipping school a couple of times with him, and lying to my parents, and being with him once in my own room on my own bed when my parents were out and had specifically forbidden me to have him over. And all the rest. But even after I repented of all these things I still did not believe for a minute that it would save me. Because you had to promise God that you were never going to do these things again or nothing would work, that was the whole idea of it. And I just couldn't promise anybody anything any more.

"If you'd let me have a rough copy of your speech to look over a day or so in advance, then," Mr. Gunther concluded. "Just a formality, of course! We know you wouldn't come out with anything inappropriate up on the speaker's platform, but we do like to have an idea what's going to be said beforehand."

"Sure, I understand," I said. I really didn't understand much at all. To me was assigned the task of telling my classmates what the past meant in terms of the future. What could I say?

Ben would know, I could ask Ben. I could tell him about everything and ask him what to do. He was flying home from Yale, finally getting home!

I began to wait for him like the Second Coming.

Chapter 11

My father went to pick him up at the airport and when they walked in the kitchen door his hair was scruffy long around his neck and ears and he had a little mustache and wire-rimmed glasses and I was never so glad to see anybody in my whole life.

"Sheena, Queen of the Jungle!" He came over and snapped my behind, which has always been his ultimate sign of affection for me. Talk about worship. As only a little sister can worship a big brother who is funny, conceited, wise, good-looking, and a terrible tease. In fact my greatest goal in life at kindergarten stage was to marry him, until that cruel day some precocious six-year-old informed me I couldn't do that, it was dirty and against the law.

"Honestly, Ben," my mother was saying. "You look awful."

"I think he looks great." Actually he did look pretty awful, but I was still glad to see him.

"See there?" He marched straight to the refrigerator and drank about half a quart of milk right from the carton and then put it back, which always drove my mother berserk. "Sheena thinks I look great. Just for that I'm going to let her unpack all my stuff and put it away."

He wasn't kidding, either. When I think of all the dirty work that boy had conned me into doing for him over the years! We hauled his stuff up to his room and after the folks finally quit hanging around he shut the door and leaned against it and stuck his tongue out of the side of his mouth.

"I see the ship models have invaded again," he said. Every time he left for Yale my mother put his old ship models back on the book shelves. "You think when I'm forty-five years old she'll still be putting the magic fleet up there?"

I wanted to tell him. All I wanted to do was make him stop joking for a minute so I could tell him the whole thing about Truck and ask him what to do, but I didn't know how to get into it.

"Hey, I brought you a present." He locked the door, dug a tin candy box out of a suitcase and lovingly unwrapped a neat little nest of joints. "Sweet friend of the weary."

"Oh, Ben." I was tempted, I really was. "I need a friend right now but believe me, that's not it."

"Oh? I thought all the teeny-boppers were turning on these days. It said so one time on the evening news." He picked one out and lit it, sucking in deeply. About half of it burned away in the first drag. He looked at it and said, "Damn Rabinovitz," then turned it around and held it out to me.

"I'm not a teeny-bopper."

"We-e-e-e-ll! Carrie Nation is alive and kicking on Bentley Road! Say now. You wouldn't call down the Feds on me my first day home, would you?"

"Smoke whatever you want, Ben. I don't care. I just think it's kind of—wasted, that's all."

"Aye, lassie, that it 'tis. Also extremely cool fun. Liberating, illuminating, non-habit forming, non-hang-over producing. *And* relaxing. So relaxing, in fact, that guess what I racked up for this last semester? One C, one D and three Incompletes."

Like it was a big joke, like I was supposed to laugh or something.

"Hey." Patting me on the head. "No sweat, kid. I'm going straight. O.K.? Right after this one, no bull. Matter of fact, I'll tell you what." He put a couple of joints in his pocket and handed the rest to me. "You can help me go straight, all right? You ought to really go for this, it's a real moral plan. Help the poor druggie pull himself up out of gutter! See this stack of typing paper? Don't let me have another single stick until you see this stack of typing paper become a twenty-page dissertation entitled 'Structure and Theme in Sir Thomas More's *Utopia*.' Fair enough?"

"That's nice, so Mother cleans house and finds this stuff in *my* room."

"Aw, Sheena. Going paranoid on me already?" Then he told me to hey, put the ship models back in the closet since he had some groovy stuff by Vonnegut and Hesse and this guy Brautigan to put on the shelves. While I did this, he would take care of the really important job, he said, which was plugging in his phonograph and putting on this ridiculous 78 rpm record, of all things, which sounded like a bunch of drunks singing.

You take the high road and I'll take the low road,
And I'll get to Scotland afore ye,
Oh me and my true love will never meet again
On the bonny, bonny banks of Loch Lo-o-o-mond!

Boy, that was all I needed.

"Latest crash hit of the Spaced-out Four Plus Five. Listen. You can hear me, I'm one of the four. Second voice from the end. Shhh." They were starting over and singing it again.

*You take the high road and I'll take the low road,
And I'll get to Scotland afore ye,
Oh me and my true love will never meet again
On the bonny, bonny banks of Loch Loo-o-o-o-mond!*

"So what's all this I hear about your new man, Sheena, Queen of the Jungle? Or maybe I should say Dale Evans, Queen of the West. Is he really a cowboy?"

It was such an abrupt opening, I couldn't think what to say.

"I should've known Daddy would fill you in on the dirt coming home from the airport. They're all upset, aren't they?"

"Yeah, you might say that."

"What did he tell you?"

"Well, to start with, he's a hot-rodder. Crummy family, no plans for an education, no plans for anything. Illiterate, crude, won't look them in the eye when they try to talk to him when he comes to pick you up. And possibly, not confirmed, in and out of trouble with the law." I sat and picked miserably at my fingernails. "So, like, what's his hidden talent?"

We were into it now but I couldn't think how to say it, and the way he was smoking that stuff I was afraid he would drift off to something else before I could get it out, and the way he was acting I wasn't so sure he'd be that much help after all.

"For pity's sake, he's not all that bad, Ben. If he was really such a total creep do you think I'd be— Really, he's just not—gray flannel suit material, that's all. And anyway, I'm the one who knows him. They don't know him. I mean, I have a good time with him, we happen to have a lot in common, but that doesn't mean—" My voice at that point sort of caught in my throat and choked out.

"He's banging you, is that what you're trying to say?"

Good old Ben. He never did mince words much. I

started crying, great mixed slobbery sobs of relief and despair.

"But it's not like *that*, it isn't like that at all—"

"I know what it's like, Jean, you don't have to tell me what it's like. I've had the pleasure a few times."

"Would you mind lowering your voice?"

"Next you'll be telling me I'm going to be *Uncle Ben* in seven months."

"Try eight," I blubbered.

"Oh, Jesus."

"I'm not really sure, I think probably my cycle is just all screwed up."

"You're screwed up, all right. Is that the newest cowboy sport around here? Just cross your fingers and uncross your legs and hope everything works out all right? You were always the one with the A's on your report card. Where's your head?"

Really *nasty*. I was sitting on his bed crying and wiping my face on a shirt or something out of his suitcase. Why did he have to be so nasty?

"I'll tell you one thing, brother, he's not a pothead! He may not be some big deal at Yale but he never once talked like that to me and he's no—he doesn't— you! You."

I fell into some fairly incoherent sobbing and the next thing I knew he was standing over me, trying to smother me, it felt like, pressing my face into his Yale T-shirt about the level of his stomach. If I hadn't been so wrapped up in my own dilemma I might have realized sooner that Ben the Magnificent wasn't doing so hot himself. There was this girl, it was such a long story, he couldn't explain, he just hoped I'd get to meet her someday, of course now he didn't know, he didn't know anything right now. Because then this other guy, and his roommate, and so many drugs. I would have to understand, it was nothing personal. A real soap opera, God he felt stupid, but he was really nowhere, drugs were nowhere, acid was insanity, speed was insanity, even pot was crap. Whole weeks lost, up in smoke, such a long story. A couple of really rough times, but he was getting himself back together now. He hadn't wanted to come home quite yet, but there was nowhere else, and anyway my graduation, so he had to come home, I would just have to understand. I couldn't tell if he was sweating or crying or stoned or what, but things were getting pretty heavy when into this sweet smoky scene came a knock upon the door.

"Ben?"

"Oh, great." He wiped a hand across his eyes, switched off the phonograph. The Spaced-out Four Plus Five *mee-uhhroooooed* into silence.

My mother tapped again. "All I want to know is, do you want chicken or liver and onions for dinner? Those are the only two things I have thawed."

Ben took a long last drag of the weed and turned to me with great solemnity. "Do you want chicken or liver and onions for dinner? Those are the only two things we have thawed."

"Chicken," I snuffled quietly. "I *hate* liver and onions." The very thought of liver and onions made fresh tears stream down my cheeks.

"We want liver and onions, Mother!" he called out in his nicest devoted-son voice. It was exactly the kind of thing Ben Travis was always doing to me, which made me feel sure that one of us, at least, was going to be all right.

It was much later, when things were quiet and straight, the dirty laundry washed and all the books lined neatly on the shelf, that Ben put on a clean shirt and came to pay me a visit. He looked at the big LOVE! poster on the back of my door and said, "Between the idea and the reality . . . falls the shadow." He was always doing that, going around quoting T. S. Eliot.

"So this guy," he said finally, after sitting down at

my desk and carefully lining up all my pens and pencils end on end. "Are you in love with him? That's the one big thing I forgot to ask."

Was I in love with him. Beautiful, Ben. "What do you want, either a yes or no?"

"Let me put it this way, would you want to marry him? I realize it's not always the same thing, but we have to start somewhere."

"It wouldn't work out with us, I guess. I believed it could for a while, but now I realize it—never would. Not with him being who he is. And me being who I am. Or who I think I'd like to be."

"But you haven't stopped seeing him."

"Well, not—yet."

"You just gathering rosebuds as long as ye may, or what?"

I didn't like the tone of that one much. "We've sort of been waiting to find out about the baby, if you really want to know."

"Baby. You mean the five-week-old blob of veins the size of a walnut? Look, Jeannie, you're bigger than it is, you decide what happens to *it,* don't let it decide what happens to *you.* I mean, Jesus, this is your *life* you're talking about!"

I sat there and fought a short, losing battle with the lump in my throat. All of a sudden Ben was developing a boundless capacity for making me cry.

"Forget about the baby for a minute. The main thing you've got to decide is what you want to do about *him.* If there's no future, there's just no future. God knows, in this life there are a lot of sweet things you can get hung up in, and the back seat of a car is just one of them. But you can't do that, you have to keep *moving.*"

It was this way he had of making things look so clear that had looked so muddled just the minute before.

"I mean, the one thing you have to do no matter what is keep moving, one way or the other, just keep moving—even if it hurts to do the smart thing, sometimes you have to do the smart thing. Starting with two little words. Like, good and bye."

"All right," I sobbed, "I know, I know, I know."

"Oh, wow. Sheena. Hey. Don't do that any more, not right now. Look, it's study-break time, how about breaking out the old stash, doling me out one little joint."

"No."

"The littlest one?"

"No chance."

"Aw, come on, Jeannie, don't be silly, I was kidding about locking it up!"

"I thought you said it wasn't habit-forming."

"It's not a habit, goddamnit, it just—makes me uptight to see girls cry."

"I'll stop crying, then." I took a couple of deep breaths and actually managed to stop crying.

Ben said a few choice words and lit a cigarette, the filter-tip mentholated kind. "All right, you self-righteous broad, where were we?"

"Sometimes you have to do the smart thing, even if it hurts."

He rubbed his hand across his eyes and said, "Yeah, now I remember." Except then he just sat there like that for about three minutes, and three minutes can be a very long time when somebody's just sitting at your desk with his forehead resting in his hand. I was thinking of calling the rescue squad, but he decided to live through it, whatever it was.

"There's this guy I know," he said finally. "I saw him today at the airport. Last year he was the biggest head on campus—he took pills, he shot speed, he dropped acid, he smoked anything that could be stuffed in a pipe and sniffed everything else. He gave me my first sugar cube, on the house. I mean, this cat had quite a following, a regular Pied Piper. So I saw him today at the airport, and I asked him what he was doing for kicks these days, just sort of friendly. And he looks at me like I'm the most ridiculous little pile of it around and says, 'I'm off all that dung, Travis, that was *last year*.' And there I stood. There stood I. I there stood. Pompous bastard, I wanted to kill him. I never wanted to kill anybody so bad in my whole life."

I waited for a second and then said gently, "Well?"

"Well. Just, well. I didn't kill him. I didn't do anything. I never do anything. I don't know anything. Ask me again next year. God, that's a happy thought, isn't it? Next year?"

Eventually we even got back to the subject at hand. Picked it up where we had left off—two little words, good and bye. Ben was right, of course, that was what had to be done. I guess for a long time I had known it, but I was finally beginning to feel it. The thing now was simply to make up my mind and do it.

"Right after graduation," I said. "I can't handle it before graduation. And not until I find out one way or the other about the—baby. We're in it together, I have to at least be able to tell him, like, true or false. You understand?"

Yeah, he understood, Ben said. And he would take me to the doctor, as soon as the graduation mess was all over with. He would go with me himself. "They'll give you a rabbit test. Then after they determine whether or not you're a rabbit—"

"You're very funny, you know that?"

"Cheer up, Jeannie, you can stand a little suspense for four or five more days. That's a nice finite period of time. And believe me, finite anxiety I would choose any day over infinite anxiety. Would you like to hear a little example of infinite anxiety? Imagine, if you can, that you're running down the middle of a street filled with open manholes and there's a giant foot behind you trying to step on you and squash you down into one of these manholes, and you're not sure what's in them but you have a pretty good idea it's water moccasins and black widow spiders. The only thing you know for sure is, the street and the manholes just keep on going forever, and the foot keeps getting closer. That's known as infinite anxiety."

I looked at him and he gave me a flat, wry smile and things started making more sense. "Spring vacation?" I said. "Was that the trip you were talking about you took over spring vacation?"

"Good memory, Sheena! Me too, good memory. Good memory must run in family."

He got up then and stretched, and started walking around looking at my books and pictures and bulletin board and things, sort of nervous, like he didn't want to bother me but didn't quite want to go yet, either.

"What's that you're doing?" he said, looking down at the blank paper I'd been sitting cross-legged in front of on my bed all this time.

"Oh, it's this silly graduation speech I told Mr. Gunther I'd give. He just made it sound like such a fantastic honor I couldn't very well say no."

"Ah. An old bureaucratic trick. So what wisdom are you unloading upon the masses?"

"I don't know, I thought you might have some ideas. Besides all that garbage about commencement marking the beginning of a new life."

"Why don't you say, 'Mr. Gunther, beloved faculty members, honored parents, and fellow graduates. You take the high road and I'll take the low road, and I'll get to—' "

"Come on, Ben, this is serious."

"Okay, how about, 'Mr. Gunther, etcetera, etcetera. In this world of ordinary people, there's one thing I want you to know: you can get about as high as you want to get, and you can go about as low as you want to go.' See? You have a little play on words there, something for everyone. Also it rhymes."

I sighed. "Everybody's grandmother will probably be there. I guess I better just tell them about commencement marking the beginning of a new life."

My period has come upon me at some pretty strange times and places, including the middle of a football field at half-time and the Library of Congress. For sheer melodrama, however, this particular set of long-awaited cramps broke all previous records by arriving just as I took my place on the speaker's platform at the Albemarle High School Fifteenth Annual Commencement Exercises, flanked by potted palms. They say emotions are the key to the whole business, and I can assure you it had been an emotional season. I could hardly restrain myself from shouting the news to Ben, whom I had spotted sitting with my folks a mere twenty-three rows back, looking extremely uncomfortable in his suit and tie and not at all interested in the Albemarle High School Fifteenth Annual Commencement Exercises.

As for my speech on "Commencement: End or Beginning?", I'm sure it was the most euphorically delivered commencement address in school history. I really don't remember much about it, myself. Afterward there was a lot of clapping, then other speeches, and what seemed like sixty thousand names being read off in their entirety, first middle and last, so that Oz became "Oswald Sheldon Rosen the Third" when his time came to step up and receive his reward for four years of faithful service, all rolled up and tied with a ribbon.

The only thing I really remember was one bad little spot in the alphabet, and I'm sure I was the only person in that whole auditorium who noticed. It came near the beginning of the H's, when Mr. Gunther skipped from Hale to Hewitt so smoothly, with such calm resonance, that you would think L. P. Hardy had never existed at all.

He wasn't there, of course. We had never even discussed his coming to see me graduate, it was one of those things we'd been trying not to think too much about. Sort of like July and August and September.

And then too, I knew how graduations always turned

into such maudlin family scenes after it was all over.

"You were wonderful!" my grandmother trilled, dabbing at her eyes. "Our little Jeannie!"

"Holy cow, yes!" Big Ben, naturally. "How did you ever think of all those stirring things to say?"

"Come stand right over here," my father was calling. He had his Polaroid, he'd only taken three rolls of me in my cap and gown already that day. "I want to get one of you standing here in front of the palm tree."

"Thank you, Gran. Gosh, thank you, everybody. Let me just go comb my hair first, Daddy. I promise, I'll be right back."

There were about a thousand girls in caps and gowns all over the ladies' room, along with their mothers and sisters and aunts, some of them laughing and some of them crying and some of them smoking cigarettes, but I finally managed to elbow my way to an empty stall. *Good old Mr. Gunther,* I thought jubilantly, *if only you knew.* About commencement marking the beginning of a new life.

Chapter 12

On our last date we took a canoe ride down the river into town to this sort of amphitheater on a barge, where different bands and orchestras gave free concerts on summer nights "under the stars." Bubba Hardy was certainly no fan of Bach or Bartok or Schubert, but he had heard about being able to go in a canoe and listen from the water like that, and he thought it was the kind of thing I would like to do. He was trying very much to please me, but the canoe trip did not turn out to be so pleasant after all because the river was so badly polluted. Where the people pulled the canoes up around the barge it was very shallow, halfway down the paddle stuck in the mucky bottom, and the water was dirty with paper and junk floating in it.

"Hard to believe this is the same river we went fishing on that day, isn't it," he said.

I hadn't said anything yet about it being our last date. It was a couple of days after graduation and he knew about my period, of course. I told him that right away, but those last two little words weren't so easy. I'd been putting it off, trying to think how best to do it. Above all I didn't want to hurt him. Ben said maybe it would be easier not to go out with him at all any more, just cut it off clean, but in this one thing I felt Ben was wrong. I felt that when a person was willing and even wanting to marry you and spend his whole life with you, the least you could do was tell him in person that you didn't even want to see him again, instead of calling him on the phone.

At the concert he moved from the seat to the bottom of the canoe, leaning his back against the seat, and I sat between his knees leaning back against him. The orchestra was playing Schubert's *Unfinished Symphony*. It sounds quite finished, it's just called the *Unfinished Symphony* because it has only two movements and most symphonies have four. I was feeling his heartbeat, wondering if it was perhaps mine instead. It was hard to tell. Planes coming into or leaving the airport roared overhead from time to time.

Some of the people in the canoes had food or beer in coolers. Some were making out, too. I envied these people who didn't give a damn, just came down and sat listening to a concert under the stars, making out in a canoe in a polluted river. I was wondering whether I should tell him right then and get it over with or wait until he took me home. I really couldn't decide what to do, when all of a sudden he decided the whole thing very neatly himself. As the old song goes, he beat me to the punch.

"Jeannie, I'm going away for a little while," was what he said. "Pop's going on a road trip for a few weeks, and he asked me to come with him, and it's what I really want to do." He was holding my hand, rubbing his thumb in a slow circle across the palm like he had done on our first date, and when I turned and looked at him, he said, "If you wanted to come with me," but just left it hanging that way, like, this is not a complete sentence. Like he already knew there was no way I was going to come with him.

"Christ, if you only knew how bad I want that.

How many times I've seen you in my head, dressed in old jeans and one of my shirts, and your hair tied back with ribbons. Miss America in the pits—handing me the wrench, polishing chrome, just being with me all the time, but—God, Jeannie. You're too good to drag around like that. You're good enough to be something yourself, not just tag along crewing for some high school dropout who might get lucky but then again might not. You might like it all right for a while, but after a while you wouldn't like it so much, and then you'd end up hating me for it. And that's something I don't want to stick around long enough to see, Jeannie. You hating me. I'm not so dumb about some things. You gotta admit, at least I always knew enough to quit while I was winning."

And the way his words came out, so quiet and smooth and all at once like that, I knew it wasn't any sudden thing with him. He'd been knowing it for a long time, too.

"I mean, I always gave you a lot of gas about saying you wanted to be a teacher, but that was just kidding, you know that. The truth is I was always proud as hell of you. From the first time I ever took you out. Because you were nice and your hair was shiny and your language was decent and your brains were in your head instead of the seat of your pants like most girls I ever knew. And I don't know what you'll end up as, you might be a doctor or a lady lawyer or just about anything, but if you want to know what I think, I think you'd make a really good teacher, you wanna know why?"

I nodded. Considering the condition of my throat right then, that was the best I could do.

"Because you don't think you know everything. Like some teachers, they know it all, you can't tell them a thing. But you, you're always right in there with your nose poked into some engine, or getting your fishing line all snagged up, or some other crazy thing, and I want you to be *good,* Jeannie. I want you to be the best goddamn teacher there ever was, or the best goddamn whatever you turn out to be."

I waited until I thought I could handle it and then I said, "Well. Thank you."

A little bit after that the concert ended. I didn't ever want it to end but that was stupid, it had to end sooner or later. So after a while it ended and the people in the canoes and amphitheater applauded. The clapping hit the water with a hollow *pock-pock-pock* sound. The conductor bowed to the audience and then to the orchestra, and the orchestra bowed to the audience, and the conductor and orchestra bowed together. Then some lights came on, and the audience on shore rose to go.

He paddled us back upstream, and I sat on the floor of the canoe, facing him. Each stroke of the paddle cut the water clean and smooth as we glided upstream in long, even surges.

"Shoot, we never went fly fishing, did we?" he said about halfway back to the dock.

"We never did a lot of things, Bubba. All those things we were going to do. So many great plans, wasted."

"Nothing is ever wasted, Teach. And don't you forget it. Nothing that ever happened between you and me was wasted."

With each stroke his arm muscles moved beneath his shirt and I looked at him all the rest of the way and thought how good and strong a person he was, and how happy he would make the right woman some day. How happy he could have made me, even, if the world was nothing but roads and river, driving during the day and camping together at night.

I just wasn't the right woman, that's all. I wasn't even any kind of woman. Doing it in the back seat of a car a few times didn't make a woman out of a girl, you had to give a lot more than that. It was childish to break things up into pieces and say I want this part but I don't want that part. To break a person up into pieces was much worse than childish, it was immoral. If I was looking for immorality, there was my immorality. I wanted his loving but I didn't want his love: that was immoral.

"So I guess this is it, huh?" he said when he pulled into my driveway at last, between those willows.

"Maybe you could—drop me a line or something."

"I don't know," he said. "I'm not too good at stuff like that."

"Well. Maybe not."

The thing to do, I thought then, was simply to get out of the car. Open the door and put one foot out and then the other foot and close the door. If I could only be cool about it, I thought. No crying or anything, just, *so long L. P., have a nice life,* and all that.

No chance.

"Hey," he said gently. "Watch out, those tears are hell on the paint job. Here. You better take this, I wanna make sure you don't get into any big trouble when I'm not around to bail you out." And he gave me the guardian angel, unhooked it from the rearview mirror and gave it to me for a souvenir. "It worked for you and it stopped working for me," he said. "And you can take that any way you want."

He didn't drag it out any, I have to give him credit for that. Just gunned his engine a couple of times, and kissed me, and told me to be good, and drove away, and never came back.

He never wrote me a letter, he never even sent me a card. I guess he really wasn't so good at stuff like that, but I watched the refrigerator door all that summer, thinking maybe he would try. I wanted to know where he was and what was happening to him, I swear that's all I wanted to know. Once in late July, I even begged Ben to drive me by the Texaco station, afraid of running into him by some long-shot chance, but with one last thing I had to know.

"Marines?" the kid on duty said. "Hell no, he didn't join the Marines. He's working at some garage up in Frederick County somewhere."

"You happy now?" Ben said.

"I guess so. He's happy, I guess that means I should be happy, right?"

He gave me one of his Walter Cronkite smiles and said, "Sometimes I wonder, Sheena. If you would have gone for him in such a big way if he wore Brooks Brothers suits and had a degree in automotive engineering and a split level in Grosse Pointe. What do you think?"

I thought I'd like to smash his hairy head in, but I didn't. I just kept watching the refrigerator door.

And one day in early August a letter did come, sure enough, but not the one I was waiting for. Two letters came, as a matter of fact, both on the same day. One was from Brenda Newman, my Darcey roommate in Richmond, Virginia. "Dear Jeannette," she wrote, "I'll bet they call you Jeannie?" She couldn't wait to get to school and meet me, she said. Was I going on the wilderness camping retreat they were having the week before registration? She wouldn't miss it for anything—the Blue Ridge should be fantastic that time of the year. She was a photography nut, she said, she even had her own darkroom at home. She knew they had darkrooms at Darcey, too—Darcey was very big on the creative arts. And P.S.: She had gotten some curtains and bedspreads for our dorm room, red-white-and-blue. Wasn't that a good antidote for pink?

But that other letter was the real killer. It was the one I had stopped waiting for so long ago, that beautiful ivied college of my choice telling me that because somebody's plans changed at the last minute, I was going to have my chance for a Holyoke education after all. I put those two letters side by side on the kitchen table and sat down and actually wept to think that life was always doing this to me, always making me choose. Looking at that letter from Mount Holyoke, I could not for the world recapture the life-or-death longing I had felt for the place only three months before. I was a different person, somehow. The prestige and tradition and solid old blueblood image, quality guaranteed, just didn't mesh with my own image of myself any more. I thought that an old renovated plantation stable would be as good a place as any to take education courses, if a person wanted to take education courses.

"It's what you do with what you've got that counts," I said a little defensively to Earl on the phone a couple of days later, trying to explain why I had written Holyoke telling them that I, too, had changed my plans. My friends were all perplexed and my mother literally speechless with dismay, but I couldn't help it. I couldn't go on forever trying to please everybody else in my life, I just had to work on satisfying myself for a while.

Earl still called a lot, and I was always very nice to him. We were good friends. One Sunday afternoon in August after Trisha had left for the beach with her family he even dropped by, just to see how I was doing. He also thought he might talk to Ben a little about school, he said.

Ben talked to him for about an hour and after Earl left he said to me, "That guy's a real bulldozer, you know? He'll probably make it big at Yale."

"Yeah, I know."

"He kind of makes your dropout cowboy friend look like a hell of a good guy."

I knew that, too.

"Do you still miss him?"

Did I still miss him.

"Even though you know it would never have worked out?"

"Yes."

"Does it seem you miss him more, or less, as time goes on?"

"More, less—God, Ben, I don't know, I just—miss him."

"Could be you're getting a little horny, too. Nothing to be ashamed of, of course," he said quickly. "Happens to the best of us. I mean, unfortunately, loving is kind of like shaving. Once you start it, you need to keep on doing it."

I pointed out the fallacy of his reasoning: he, for instance, was growing a beard.

"Yes, that's true, Sheena. You could always grow a beard."

He could drive you absolutely crazy, Ben Travis could. Very easily. He got a job working in construction that summer and he would come home tired and hairy and sweaty at night and drink a beer and go to sleep in front of the TV with Stanley curled up under his arm, and he made me wish I was a boy instead of a girl. I wished I could be a boy and work in construction and go around laying girls here and there and not giving a damn about whether I loved them or not.

And I wished I had the nerve to drive out to Broom Creek once more all by myself and watch Truck from the stands without him knowing it. Maybe he would look raunchy to me or I would see him pick his nose or something when he thought nobody was looking. I just wished I could watch him lose a few races or be a bad sport for a change. I thought that might help a little.

I would go to the pool on hot summer days and look at the long-haired lifeguards in tight swim trunks, all tanned and muscled across their chests and legs, and I would think about how it had been with Truck, and wonder how it would be with them. And I thought how hard it was to be only seventeen and already missing a boy that way. It made me wonder what I would be like when I was eighteen, or nineteen, or twenty.

Sometimes I wished I had never even met him and none of it had happened, not Slave Day or fishing or drag racing or any of it, but of course I didn't really wish that. And even if I did, what good was that now? It had simply *been,* that's all—for better or worse—and nothing could ever make it un-be, ever. Two roads diverged in a yellow wood and I picked one of the roads and what the hell good did it do to sit around wondering about the other? Because the minute I picked the one, the other ceased to exist, that's just the way it worked.

So at the end of all this wishing, I came back to the little thing he had said to me in the canoe that night, about nothing between us ever being wasted. I thought if I could only keep thinking of it that way then surely I would know what it had all meant some day.

"Because everything must mean something," I said to Ben one evening out on the patio just as it was getting dark. "You know?" That bad time of the day, the time the drags would just be breaking up out at Broom Creek. "Even if it hurt me some. Or changed me some. At least I have to believe that I found out a lot of things about myself, and him, and other things, and other people, but mostly myself—that I wouldn't have found out for a long time. Maybe even never."

Ben took off his glasses and wiped one lens on his shirt very carefully and then wiped the other lens very carefully and put them back on and said, "Join the club." And for once he wasn't clowning, for that I was grateful. With Ben there was always something to be grateful for.

ABOUT THE AUTHOR

DONIA WHITELEY MILLS has lived in many sections of the United States, first as the daughter of a naval officer, and then for two years after she was married, while her husband was in the army. She is a graduate of Wake Forest University, and received an M.A. from the University of Pennsylvania.

Donia Mills published her first short story when she was fourteen years old, and since then has continued to write stories and articles that have appeared in numerous magazines. Her first novel for young people was *The Rules of the Game*.

Mrs. Mills lives with her husband, their small daughter, and two beagles in Silver Spring, Maryland.